Praise for *Stay*

Texas Bluebonnet Award Winner

"A small dog, the elderly woman who owns him,
and a homeless girl come together to create a tale
of serendipity. Entrancing and uplifting."
—*Kirkus Reviews* (starred review)

"Evoking innocent and energetic doggy-ish dedication,
love, and longing. This title is an excellent book for
raising awareness and empathy."
—*School Library Journal*

"Timely, important, and truly beautiful."
—Katherine Applegate,
Newbery Medal–winning author

ALSO BY BOBBIE PYRON

A Dog's Way Home

A Pup Called Trouble

BOBBIE PYRON

Stay

KATHERINE TEGEN BOOKS
An Imprint of HarperCollins Publishers

Library of Congress Control Number: 2018968550
ISBN 978-0-06-283923-7

Typography by Molly Fehr
20 21 22 23 24   PC/BRR   10 9 8 7 6 5 4 3 2 1
❖
First paperback edition, 2020

To the girls of Girl Scout troop 6000.
You are our future; you are my inspiration.

Stay

∾ 1 ∾

Piper

I rest my head against the cold window of the Country-Wide bus, watching the world go by. The full moon lights up empty fields. Cornstalks and stubble throw long shadows across the ground. It's pretty and kind of mysterious too.

To tell you the truth, I think I'm the only person on the entire bus who's awake. Well, except for the driver, but I can't see her anyway. Her name tag said Doreen. She seems nice.

Across the aisle, my little brother, Dylan, sleeps with his head in Mama's lap. His red superhero cape is spread across his body. It's just an old red blanket he won't give up without pitching a royal fit, so we pretend it gives him superpowers, especially when his asthma is bad. I can just see the tips of his sneakers peeking out from under the blanket. He has his best friend, Ted the stuffed shark, tucked under his chin.

I gaze back out the window at the headlights of cars ticking by; at the warm yellow porch lights glowing outside of houses in the neighborhoods we pass. Like our old neighborhood and our little house.

Thinking of home reminds me of the things in the backpack by my feet. Inside, along with my Firefly Girls sash, a jacket, and some other stuff, is my favorite book, *My Side of the Mountain*. I could take it out and read it—again—but if I turn on the overhead light, it'll wake Daddy up.

Daddy snores lightly, almost like a purr, in the seat beside me. I lean my head against his arm and feel warm skin through the thin flannel shirt. I can smell his familiar scent of cigarettes and Juicy Fruit gum. And if I rub my nose just a little deeper into the soft flannel, I swear I can smell the salty sea air of home.

I close my eyes. The bus rocks so, so gently as it speeds through the night past farms and fields and towns, houses and neighborhoods, everyone sleeping snug as bugs in their beds.

Since I can't read my book, I decide to run my favorite "imaginary movie" in my head. I'm not the world's best sleeper, especially when I worry, which is pretty much most of the time. So when I can't sleep, I make up movies. My favorite is *Trudeau Family Wins*

Big! In it, we win the lottery and have all the things we've ever wanted: a house on the water and a big boat for Daddy, a fenced-in yard with a dog for me, college for Mama, and a brand-new bicycle for Dylan. And best of all, no worries about paying the bills.

I smile just a tiny bit. My mind latches onto the rhythm of the rocking bus. It whispers in time, over and over, "Maybe, maybe, maybe . . ."

∽ 2 ∽

Baby and Jewel

A small brown dog listens
to the beat of his world
in the chest of a woman
named Jewel.
He watches a raccoon waddle across the grass
in the bright moonlight.
Baby squirms with curiosity.
Is it doggish?
Is it cattish?
Oh! So many things to smell!
To see!
To make friends with!
Jewel stirs.
Baby settles
against her chest
quiet

a good, good dog.
He tucks his head beneath her chin.
Jewel's scent fills every inch
of the little dog
with deep joy.
Baby and Jewel
a pack of two
warm and safe together.

3

Somewhere

"Time to wake up, Piper."

I sit up and blink at the sunlight filling the bus. Outside the windows are tall, tall buildings, rushing traffic, trash pushed up against the sidewalk curbs by the wind. What happened to the moonlit fields? The tidy neighborhoods?

Daddy lifts his Atlanta Braves cap from his head and runs his fingers through his hair.

"You sleep okay, little chicken?" he asks around a yawn.

I yawn too. "I guess. The moon was awful bright."

Everybody's waking up now. They stand and begin gathering their bags, boxes, backpacks, and suitcases from under seats and overhead racks.

Mama gives me a tired smile as she shifts Dylan

from one arm to the other. "Morning, sweetheart." She stretches and tries to smooth her shirt. Her hair is coming loose from its braid.

"Your hair's a mess, Mama," I say. "Let me fix it."

I undo her braid, smooth down her springy hair as best I can, and rebraid it nice and tight.

"Thanks, honey," she says. She scoops Dylan up off the seat and into her arms. Dylan can sleep through anything. Once he slept through a tornado that hit near our street. Never made a sound. Me, I'm not much of a sleeper. I'm like Daddy that way.

Dylan's eyes open. I watch as he slowly comes back to the world. His eyes are the same deep, deep sea blue as Mama's.

"Where are we?" he asks in his croaky little voice.

I look back out the windows. Nothing looks familiar. Nothing looks like anywhere we've been. And we've been a lot of places over the last few months.

I reach out and push the hair out of his eyes. His face is hot and damp. For just a second, I let my fingers rest against his cheek.

"Somewhere," I answer. "We're somewhere."

"Over the rainbow?" Dylan asks. Me and Dylan used to watch *The Wizard of Oz* every Easter when it came on TV, and we can sing every song.

I smile and click my red high-top tennis shoes

three times. "Maybe."

Mama hands me Dylan's SpongeBob backpack, his red superhero cape, and Ted the Shark. I sling my backpack over one shoulder, Dylan's over the other.

We step off the bus. Mama sets Dylan on the ground while she checks to make sure we have everything. Two suitcases and one duffel bag.

I look around and up. I've never seen so many people and so many tall buildings. Even when we stayed with Mama's cousin in Baton Rouge, it wasn't like this.

"Look, Piper!" Dylan grabs my hand and clutches it hard. There, off in the distance, are mountains so high, they look like they've surely punched a hole right through the sky and into heaven. I feel myself light up inside. Ever since I read *My Side of the Mountain*, I've wanted to see the mountains. Be *on* a mountain like Sam Gribley.

I squeeze his hand. Just like Dorothy when she first sees Munchkinland, I say, "Toto, I don't think we're in Kansas anymore."

4

A New Day

"Oh Lord, let me get these old bones moving
one more day."
Jewel says this each and every morning
as she stretches her legs
arms
fingers
back.
Baby wags his bit of a tail
and pulls back his lips in a toothy smile
as he does every morning.
A frisky breeze
skitters across the grass, bringing
delicious scents
to Baby's nose.
The sweet smell of rotting leaves.

The bitter smell of acorns.
The musky smell of squirrels.
Squirrels!
Baby runs tight circles
around and around and around Jewel,
yipping with delight.
A brand-new day to see old friends
and make new ones.
A new day to explore the city with Jewel.
Always with Jewel.
What could be better?
Baby does not understand why sometimes
the smell of sadness and confusion
spools from Jewel.
Like now.
Baby twirls and spins
on back legs.
Jewel laughs.
She lifts Baby and kisses the white patch
on the top of his head.
A patch shaped like a snowflake.
"Look, Baby," Jewel says. "Just look at the world."
And Baby does.
Trees, swings, picnic tables, a pond,
wet leaves carpeting the ground and
in the distance

tall buildings
and farther still,
mountains.
Baby licks Jewel's chin and squirms in her arms.
Let's go!

∽ 5 ∽

Signs

Outside the bus station the wind is cold. It seems like the farther we've traveled from home, the colder it is.

"This just doesn't make any sense." Daddy looks at the piece of paper in his hand, then up at the street signs, then back at the paper. "Three Hundred Eighty-Six West, Two Hundred South," he reads out loud. He shakes his head. "What the heck kind of address is that?"

"I'm cold," Dylan whimpers.

Mama wraps Dylan's red blanket tight around his shoulders and strains to pick him up. Mama's kind of small, so it's not easy for her to lift him anymore.

I pull my denim jacket out of my pack. "You're not a little baby, you know," I snap at Dylan. Right away, I feel bad.

Dylan pops his thumb into his mouth and looks at the mountains.

Mama frowns. "I seem to remember, young lady, you asking to be held when you were five."

I turn away to pull on my jacket. I don't want her to see me try to swallow past the lump in my throat. I don't want her to know that even though I'm almost twelve now, I'd give anything to climb right into her lap. Or Daddy's. I quickly touch my Firefly Girls sash in the bottom of my pack for comfort, then zip it up.

Doreen, the bus driver lady, comes over to Daddy, still puzzling over the paper. "Can I help you?" she asks. She's almost as tall as Daddy, which is saying something.

Daddy holds out the paper to her. "This is the address I have for where we're going, but I can't make sense of it."

Doreen studies the address, then looks over at Mama holding Dylan. "I see," she says. She clears her throat. "You're going two blocks that way north"— she points—"and then you'll turn west—left—and go three blocks. You'll see the sign."

"Thank you," Daddy says.

Doreen nods and heads back to the Country-Wide Travel bus. She pauses before she climbs the stairs. "Good luck to you," she calls.

"Okay, let's get going then." Daddy slings the duffel bag over one shoulder and grabs the heaviest of the two suitcases.

Mama sets Dylan down. She threads his arms through the loops of his SpongeBob backpack. "Time to be a big boy now," she says, handing him his stuffed shark.

I pull my backpack on. I take Dylan's hand. "Let's go, Toto," I say. I hold on to his little hand like a lifeline to normal.

We walk and walk and walk and walk.

After a while, Dylan whines, "I'm tired, Daddy. When will we be there?"

I see Daddy's shoulders tense under his thin flannel shirt.

"Let's play I spy," I say.

Before Dylan can complain any more, I say, "I spy with my own little eye something yellow and black with big wheels."

"School bus!" he yips, pointing at the bus waiting at the red light.

I squeeze his hand. "Good job. Your turn."

Dylan looks around. He smiles and gives a little hop. "I spy with my own little eyes something small and brown and furry."

Sure enough, there on a corner of the intersection

stands a woman in a flowery dress holding up a cardboard sign. The sign says "Hungry! Please help!" Beside her sits a little brown dog with white paws and a white patch on its head. The dog looks straight at me and wags its stubby tail. The woman looks desperate, but the dog looks as happy as can be. I wish I could be like that little dog.

Dylan tugs on my hand. "Did you guess?"

I tear my eyes away from the woman and dog. "Yeah," I say, hurrying to catch up with Daddy. "A dog."

We keep playing as we follow Daddy through the city. I spy something big and green and overflowing with garbage. Dylan spies something silver and square with four small wheels: an abandoned shopping cart. Someone sleeps next to it right on the sidewalk. I pull Dylan closer and hurry past.

"Daddy, I'm hungry," Dylan complains.

"We're almost there, buddy," Daddy says. Again.

Behind me, I hear Mama sigh.

Finally, Daddy stops. He looks down at the paper, then up at the sign. "This must be it," he says in a voice so low I can barely hear him.

I look up at the sign. My heart drops fast, like at the very top of a roller coaster.

Mama comes up and stands beside me. She takes

my empty hand. We both stand there looking up at the sign like it's in some kind of foreign language.

"What does it say?" Dylan asks.

I look over at Mama. This can't be right, can it?

Reading my thoughts, she looks away and blinks fast.

I take a gulp of air. "It says Sixth West Emergency Shelter."

Dylan frowns and shifts his toy shark in his arms. "What's a 'mergency shelter?"

I want to say it's a place where people go who don't have a home, but I don't.

Mama runs her hand over Dylan's curly hair sticking up all kind of ways. "It's like a hotel, honey." She looks at me and puts her hand on my shoulder. "It'll be fine."

But how can it? Every place we've been since we lost our home four months ago, every possibility that didn't work out, has made our world feel smaller. I never realized until it was gone how something as normal as hope lights up your world.

∾ 6 ∾

Good Folks,
Bad Folks

Baby stands at their corner with Jewel,
watching the traffic go one way
and then the other,
stop and go,
then stop again.
Where are they going? he wonders.
He remembers riding in cars, on a bus.
Outside
in the wide-open world
is better.
Inside some cars
a thump, thump, thump
makes the inside of Baby's ears beat like a drum.
Inside some cars

children press their faces,
sticky fingers, hands, and noses,
against the car windows.
They point, stare, and wave.
Baby yips hello, wags his bit of a tail.
Jewel holds up her sign. The wind tugs at the hem of
    her dress.
"Please help," she calls. "Please help me and Baby."
At the sound of his name, the little brown dog
leaps
and twirls on his back legs
like leaves in the wind.
A window rolls down.
An arm sticks out holding
a dollar, maybe two.
"Bless you," Jewel says.
Baby yips his thanks and spins in a circle of delight.
Another window rolls down.
Another hand holds out hope.
The light blinks.
The cars go.
Baby watches a crow fly overhead
with something in its beak.
"Bum!" someone yells from a yellow car.
"Get a job!" another someone yells from a black car.
Jewel wipes at her face.
Her smell of fear and despair

makes Baby want to run, run, run
after those cars and bite them.
A woman threads her way through the waiting traffic
and steps onto their corner.
She hands Jewel a delicious-smelling something
wrapped up warm and tight.
She touches Jewel's shoulder.
She pats Baby on the head with a hand
that smells like flowers.
"Good boy," she says. "Good, good boy."
Baby sneezes in agreement
as the woman with the flower hands
walks away.
Jewel unwraps the paper.
The joyous smell of cheese, butter, meat
fills the little dog's nose.
Rapture! He barks.
Jewel tears the sandwich,
puts half on the ground for Baby.
"Remember this, Baby," Jewel says.
Baby cocks his head to one side and listens.
"There are good folks out there."
"Some bad folks, but mostly good."
"Don't ever forget, Baby. Mostly good."
Baby licks his white paws
over and over and over
tasting every last crumb.

∾ 7 ∾

Divided

"What do you mean, I can't stay with my family?"
Daddy asks for maybe the millionth time. His
voice is a notch higher than the last time he asked.

Dylan clutches Daddy's leg. My heart pounds in
panic.

"I'm sorry, Mr. Trudeau, but that's the rule at the
emergency shelter," the woman behind the desk explains.
"Women and children stay in this building, and men in
the shelter next door. It's for security reasons."

I look at Mama. Surely she can fix this. Mama is
famous for her negotiation skills. Grandpa Bill used to
say Mama could talk the chicken right off the bone.

But Mama's eyes fill with tears. Her nose is red.
She's clutching and unclutching the handle of the
suitcase.

My grandma Bess used to say, the hotter the water, the stronger the tea. Let me tell you, right now the Trudeau family is in a heck of a lot of hot water.

I take a deep breath, stick my chin out, and say real importantly, "Our family has to stay together, ma'am." I hope she can't see my knees knocking. I look at her name tag. "Becky," I add.

Becky's eyes soften. "I wish you could, truly I do, but those are the rules."

Becky pushes a form across her desk. "Why don't you start filling this out," she says, tapping the paper with her fingernail, "while I get a few things you'll need." She smiles and nods. "Then we'll get you all settled. You'll feel better after that."

"Oh," she says, pulling out another form. "Fill this one out too. It's for Hope House, a family shelter. We'll get you on their waiting list right away, so you can all be together."

Hope House. I like the sound of that.

Daddy bends low over the desk to fill out the forms. I swallow hard and stroke Dylan's hair. A fluorescent light buzzes overhead. I can smell fried onions and Pine-Sol cleaner. Down a long hallway, a baby cries.

Becky returns with two plastic bags. She hands one to Mama and one to Daddy. "Towels, blankets, toiletries, things to help you settle in," Becky explains.

Dylan whimpers a tear-laced, watery sniff.

"Oh, I almost forgot." Becky kneels down in front of Dylan and hands him a paper bag. She smiles. "Some things just for you."

"Really?" Dylan opens the bag. Inside are coloring books, crayons, puzzle games on sheets of paper, and a paperback book.

"Look!" he says, holding out the bag like it's trick-or-treat. "Just for me!"

Becky looks right into my eyes. "I'm sure you're a wonderful big sister and will help him enjoy his treats."

I nod. "Yes, ma'am."

"Mr. Trudeau," Becky says in a gentle but firm voice, "you head on over to the men's shelter. They'll get you all settled into a nice room."

Becky touches Mama's arm. "Let me show you around."

Dylan takes my hand. "I'll share my crayons with you," he says, smiling up at me.

I straighten the superhero cape on his shoulders. "Thanks," I say. "I'll read that book to you, if you want."

"Yay!" Dylan skips between me and Mama as we walk down a long hallway lined with doors, some open, some closed.

I remember Daddy. He's standing there looking

lost. I raise my free hand and wave.

"We'll be back, Daddy!" I call.

As we walk down the hall, I try not to look inside the rooms that have open doors. I know it's rude, but I can't help it. My curiosity gets the best of me.

Inside one room, a woman sits on her cot writing in a notebook.

Next door, a lady holds a tiny baby close to her chest, rocking it back and forth.

Inside another room, a woman runs a comb through a girl's long black hair while two little boys play with cars at her feet. The girl looks at me and smiles. I smile back and hurry after Mama.

"You're lucky," Becky says as she stops in front of a closed door all the way at the end of the hall. "This room has a nice, big window." I see in my mind the tall, sun-filled windows in our house back home.

Becky pulls out a ring with about a million keys on it. She slips a key in the lock and pushes open the door.

At first, I don't see the window. I see two cots piled with blankets and pillows, an old chest of drawers, and a chair. That's it.

Then I see it: a small window high above our heads. I hear Becky telling Mama about the bathroom down the hall and what time they lock the shelter doors at night and where the community dining room is.

But I'm looking at the piece of blue outside the window and wondering how this can be the same sky, the same piece of blue, I knew back home.

∽ 8 ∽

Fancy Dog

Later
in their park
under a sun-dappled sky,
Baby sees a fancy dog,
a live-inside kind of dog.
Baby sees this dog almost every day.
Every day
the fancy dog and her person
come from the exact same direction
at the exact same time,
the dog leading the way, tail up,
tongue out
with anticipation.
They walk the same path through the cottonwood
    trees,

circle the duck pond twice,
then stop at the same bench where they always stop
and sit.
Baby remembers how it was to live in the same place,
take the same walk, see the same things
every day.
"Our home is everywhere!" Baby yips with happiness.
Parks. Streets.
Inside tumbledown buildings.
And now in this park, full of delicious smells
and friends:
Ree and Ajax
Linda and Duke
Jerry and Lucky.
"We are always together now, always
me and my Jewel."
The fancy dog's person unclips the leash from the
    dog's collar.
The collar sparkles like dew on grass.
The dog cocks her head,
considers the delights held
in a mud puddle.
Baby runs through the puddle, splashing mud
on the fancy dog's perfect white coat.
The not-as-fancy-now dog's person frowns.
She clips the leash on the sparkly collar.

Baby does not understand leashes.
Jewel walks, Baby walks beside her.
Jewel tells Baby to stay, he stays.
Why would he do anything else?
Baby hears the fancy dog sigh.
He watches as the dog and her person
walk the same path
through the cottonwood trees,
past the swings
back the way they always go.
But now,
the fancy dog walks behind,
feet dragging,
tail down.
Baby feels sad for the fancy dog until
he hears Jewel call, "Let's go, Baby."
Baby's heart leaps. His two favorite words!
New places, new people,
one lucky dog.

∽ 9 ∽

We All Look Up

Let me tell you, living in a shelter means you spend a lot of time standing in line and waiting. First, we stand in line and wait to take showers, then we wait to wash and dry our clothes. Mama says it's a good way to meet people, though. Back home, when we'd go to the Piggly Wiggly to do our grocery shopping, by the time we got to the checkout lady, Mama was best friends with everybody in line. And she loved going to the Just Like Home Laundromat to catch up on all the town gossip.

Here, though, people don't seem so friendly or talkative.

By the time we get ourselves and our clothes clean, there's a new lady at the front desk. Her name is Jean. She smiles a lot. She gives us meal tickets for the Sixth

Street Community Kitchen. "It's nothing fancy, but it'll fill you up," she says with a laugh. She also gives us directions to the Christian Center, where we can get winter coats, gloves, and hats. "Just show them this," she says, handing Mama a slip of paper with a bright-green stamp on it, "and they'll let you pick out a few things for free. Can't beat that!" Jean has a lot of enthusiasm for her job.

We meet Daddy out front. Dylan wraps his arms around Daddy's legs like he's never going to let go. Daddy looks so tired. My heart hurts. I go stand next to him, touch the sleeve of his jacket. "Hey, Daddy," I say.

Daddy gives me a quick, sideways hug. "Hey, peanut," he says. "Take your little brother's hand." Gently, he peels Dylan's arms from his legs.

We wait in line for the right bus to take to the Christian Center. I don't mind the waiting in this line so much. I love looking at those high, faraway mountains.

When we finally get to the Christian Center, we wait, again, while the guy working there unlocks the back room. Mama hands him the piece of paper with the bright-green stamp while Daddy tries to keep Dylan from running in and out of the clothes racks.

The man pushes open the door. "Here you go," he says.

Mama's face falls just the tiniest bit. No nice, neat clothes racks in here. Instead, clothes piled up in boxes without rhyme or reason. The room smells like mothballs and bleach.

Mama pulls a smile out of her pocket anyway. "Thank you," she says.

I've never had a real winter coat, and only hats and gloves for fun. We never needed much more than a heavy sweater in Louisiana. After digging through two tall boxes, I find a red wool coat with a hood and pockets. "It's perfect," Mama says. "The red shows off your pretty blond hair and green eyes." Describing my hair as blond is a bit of a stretch—it's more light brown—but that's okay. My eyes are, for a fact, green.

After we've gotten our coats, hats, and gloves, Daddy says we should walk around and "get the lay of the land." He said this same thing in Tallahassee, where his buddy Jim had promised him a job; in Baton Rouge, when we stayed with Mama's cousin; and in Abilene, Texas, where our car broke down. For good. And where Dylan landed in the emergency room with bad asthma, which used up almost all our money.

The wind blows hard and cold. I pull my hood up and take the gloves out of my coat pocket. A little slip of paper flutters to the sidewalk. I pick it up.

It's from a fortune cookie. It says "The stranger you will meet will become your friend." I snort. I show it to Mama. "Everybody here is a stranger," I say. Back home, between school and my Firefly Girls troop, I had lots of friends. And the town was so small, there were hardly any strangers.

"Yes, but every stranger you meet is a friend in disguise," she says, looping her arm through mine and bumping me with her hip.

We stand in line again, waiting, for the Sixth Street Community Kitchen to open. At least Daddy gets to go inside and eat with us. Mama's talking with a woman behind us who has a little baby with a runny nose. Daddy's frowning at the Help Wanted ads in the newspaper. Dylan is just about worn completely out, so I keep him close to me and pull his new hat down over his ears.

There are lots of people in this line waiting to eat. Some have big packs on their backs, some push shopping carts loaded with all kinds of stuff. There are old people who don't talk much (unlike the old people back home), and women telling their kids to behave. People talking, some laughing, bare hands rubbing together to keep warm. The wind carries the smell of buttered bread and unwashed clothes.

Other people—people looking like they have somewhere important to go—don't look at us. They don't want to get too close, like our situation—standing in a line to eat—might be catching. I shrink inside my coat. I'm glad everybody here is a stranger.

I see the girl with the long black hair from the shelter ahead of us. She smiles and waves.

I'm just about to wave back when the woman in front of us turns around.

Her silver hair blows in the wind. Where have I seen her?

"Have you seen Sis?" she asks. Her blue eyes dart with worry. Her eyes, the color anyway, remind me of Grandma Bess.

"Um, I'm not sure who Sis is, ma'am," I answer.

The old woman looks up at the sky. "The Angels are coming in their chariots of wind and ice," she says.

Okay, that's kind of weird. Before I can answer, I see something wiggle under the woman's coat. A little brown, fuzzy head pops out under the woman's chin. The dog looks right at me and, I can tell by the way his eyes smile, he's wagging his tail.

"Oh my gosh, he's so cute!" I say.

The worry leaves the woman's eyes. She smiles. "This is my Baby," she says.

The little dog tips his head up and licks her chin.

"Can I pet him?" I whisper.

The woman nods. "Dogs are the best medicine," she says.

I reach out and stroke the top of his head. It's warm beneath my hand. He closes his eyes and makes an almost-purring sound of contentment.

I know exactly how he feels. Just for that moment, everything feels normal, even good. My heart is light.

A voice behind us breaks the spell. "Line's moving."

I blink. I'm standing in the cold, waiting to eat.

I put my hand in my pocket to hold on to that good feeling of the little dog's head.

"Thank you, ma'am," I say. "I do feel better."

She turns back around. In my mind, I'm already planning on sharing my food—whatever it is—with that dog.

Then I hear a voice at the front of the line say, "Come on, Jewel, you know the rules. You can't come in with your dog."

"Please, Rick," she pleads with the man at the door, "just this one time. He won't hurt anybody. Why," she says all in a rush, "you won't even know he's there."

The man named Rick shakes his head. "I'm sorry, Jewel." He motions for the next person in line to come through the door.

"It's not fair," I mutter.

"It's mean," Dylan says, rubbing his eyes.

The old woman walks toward us. Her eyes are fixed on the sidewalk. She's saying something over and over that I can't hear. But oh! That little dog, Baby, looks directly into my eyes. Like he has all the hope in the world. And for just a minute, for the first time in a long time, I feel a little flicker of hope too.

Miss Jean was right: the food was not very good—canned corn, canned green beans, soupy potatoes, some kind of meat, sliced white bread—but it did fill us up.

As we walk back to the shelter, even though it's colder than ever and the wind pushes us along the sidewalk, we're all dragging our feet. We know we have to get back by eight or we'll be locked out, but getting back also means Daddy goes one way and we go the other.

Then, all of a sudden, Dylan stops dead in his tracks. He looks up into the streetlight. "Look!" he cries.

I can't make sense of what I'm seeing. White, white feathery things swirling, cartwheeling down from the black night sky. At first there's just a few, and I wonder if I imagined it. Then there's more and more, like swarms of white butterflies.

Something wet and cold lands on my cheek. I gasp. "Snow!"

Dylan laughs. He runs this way and that, trying to catch the snowflakes in his hand just like he used to chase fireflies at home.

Mama turns her face to the sky, closes her eyes, and smiles a beautiful smile. "Snow." She sighs with happiness.

Daddy puts his arm around her and, for the first time in forever, he smiles too.

We all look up at the wonder of it in the circle of light. Snowflakes swirling, landing, touching cheeks, noses, eyelashes like little kisses from heaven.

∽ 10 ∽

Listen, Baby Says

The smell of sadness surrounds Baby
inside the warmth of Jewel's coat.
His heart beats in time
with her footsteps
as they walk up one street and down another.
Past the place where people sleep inside
not outside
like Baby and Jewel.
He can smell the longing in her heart.
"Listen," Baby says, nudging her with his head,
"listen to the wind in the trees,
the song. We have that."
Across the street, Baby smells the tumbledown
    building
where they slept

when they first came to this city.
That memory leads Baby back to the feel of the
  rocking bus
and the hum of the wheels against the road
as he lay curled
hidden
in the bottom of Jewel's bag.
Curled up in sweaters, socks, a coat,
a little brown bunny missing one eye,
his favorite toy.
The old leather book that holds the smell of Jewel's
  hands,
the book she reads over and over and over
when she's sad or afraid or
jubilant.
The smaller book she never opens anymore.
The light changes.
The cars stop.
A cold wind blows.
Baby feels Jewel's heart shudder.
"Listen," Baby says as he licks the wet, salty tears
from the deep furrows on his Jewel's face.
"There is nothing between the world
and us."
Baby feels Jewel's heart lift.
She looks up into the street light.

She laughs,
closes her eyes
and spins in slow circles
as snowflakes wheel down and around them.
"Oh Baby, my Baby," she sings over and over
into his waiting ear.
"What a wonderful world."
The light changes again.
The cars creep forward,
tires spin,
as the woman and dog
dance in the snow light.

∽ 11 ∽

Just Piper

When I wake up this morning, the first thing I do is look outside the little window. The light is gray. Snow pecks against the glass, making tiny ticking sounds. Everything is white.

Down in the lobby, breakfast stuff is lined up on two long tables. Mama makes us each drink a small carton of milk before we can have a doughnut. Dylan cries when Mama tells him he can have two bananas but not two doughnuts. I bet Daddy gets to eat all the doughnuts he wants over at his shelter.

Thinking about Daddy makes me sad.

I hear Mama say, "Oh no, we don't need to apply for food stamps. We've just hit a little rough patch, that's all."

This patch we've been in for the last four months seems like a football field full of briars if you ask me.

But no one does. Or has.

I feel a light touch on my arm. It's the girl with the long black hair.

"Hi," she says, smiling with powdered-sugar-dusted lips.

"Hi," I say.

"You're new here, right?"

"Yes," I say. "We came here from Abilene, Texas, but," I add, "I was born and raised in Louisiana."

She nods. "We came from a town north of here. We've been here for one week and four days."

I think about Mama sleeping on the floor between our two cots and the tiny window and the mouse droppings behind the wooden chair and Daddy living across the street. A week feels like a very long time.

"We won't be here that long," I say, glancing over at Mama. She's got storm clouds in her eyes. Not a good thing.

The girl with the long black hair sips her juice box and nods. "We're hoping to get in the family shelter any day now. Maybe we can be friends there."

Mama grabs Dylan's hand and marches over in our direction. I hear myself say what I've heard Daddy say a million times over the last few months: "We won't be staying here long. We'll be moving on to something better with more opportunities soon."

Or the best thing, go back home.

Mama gives the girl a tight smile, then says to me, "Breakfast is over. Your brother can't be trusted around doughnuts." Dylan hangs his head and sniffles.

The girl smiles. "Brothers," she says. "You're lucky you just have one."

I roll my eyes.

Halfway across the lobby, she calls, "My name's Gabriela, by the way. Gabby for short."

"My name's Piper. Just Piper."

After Mama gets Dylan cleaned up, we bundle into our coats and gloves and hats and meet Daddy out front. Dylan leaps into Daddy's arms with a yip. I wish I could too. Instead I just say, "Hey, Daddy."

He reaches out and pulls me to him. "Hey, chicken. You doing okay?"

"I'm okay, Daddy," I say against his new coat. It already smells like him.

Daddy lifts Dylan up and up onto his shoulders while we wait for the bus. "I can see the whole world!" Dylan sings.

I take off a glove and run my hand over the snow resting on the bench. It's cold and wet and melts as soon as I touch it. I bring my fingers to my lips to taste the snow.

"Piper," Daddy says, frowning down at me. He

shakes his head. "It's dirty."

But how could something so white, so new, be dirty? I take off my other glove and, not looking at him, bury my hand beneath the snow.

We spend all day standing in lines.

Lines at the employment office and lines at the unemployment office.

Dylan ate too many doughnuts at breakfast, so he has the sugar crazies. I about wear myself completely out trying to keep him from turning everything upside down and getting us kicked out.

Then we walk three blocks through the wet, cold snow to wait in another line at the Department of Human Services.

My red high-tops have turned into popsicles. Dylan's sugar's worn off and turned him into a screaming, whining meemie. I try my best to distract him with I spy, but it doesn't work. At all.

By the time we get to the front of the line, most of Mama's hair has come loose from her braid and Daddy has a twitch in his eyelid.

I am almost asleep on my feet when I hear my mother say in a voice I've never heard, "You've got to be kidding me!" My eyes pop open.

Mama's face goes red, then white. She's quivering

all over. I haven't seen her look like this since Grandma Bess's funeral.

The woman behind the glass divider taps a sign taped to the window with her red fingernail. "It says right here: children under the age of sixteen must have birth certificates in order to apply for general assistance."

Mama looks at the woman like she has two heads. Then I see something shift in Mama's eyes.

"Look," she says. "I understand the need for the rules, I really do." Mama leans in closer and puts on her best practical voice. "And I know you're doing the *best* job you can"—she glances at the woman's name tag—"Mrs. Fulton."

I relax just a little. Mama will get this straightened right out.

"But," Mama continues, nodding to us, "we've never been in this situation before. All we want is for our babies to be safe and warm, with food in their bellies. The last thing on my mind was birth certificates." She blinks back real tears. "You can understand that, can't you?"

The woman sighs. She taps the sign again, a little less enthusiastically this time. "Sorry," she says. "Those are the rules."

If Daddy weren't holding a sleeping Dylan, I think

his fist would go right through that glass.

The woman leans to the side and looks around Mama. "Next!"

It's snowing again. I think I still like snow, but not the cold. I pull the hood up on my coat and trudge through the slush to the bus stop. We'll wait in line again to eat our supper at the Sixth Street Community Kitchen. I'm so hungry and cold and tired even canned green beans with their weird squeak and that gray goopy gravy sound good right about now. I feel snow sting my cheeks and tears sting my eyes.

I look around for that old woman and her little dog, Baby. I sure could use a dose of dog medicine right about now.

Then something catches my attention: It's a flyer stapled to a pole. At the top of the flyer it says in big letters "Firefly Girls Troop 423 Meets Tonight!" I stop and look at the smiling girls on the flyer. I don't bother reading what it says, I just look at those big smiles, shining eyes, and familiar electric-blue-and-yellow uniforms. I loved being a Firefly Girl. I loved the songs and crafts and field trips. I loved earning pins and badges. And I was the best, top-earning gourmet brownie seller in our troop back home in Cyprus Point. But most of all, I loved the friends I made, being part of something.

The bus pulls up, splashing cold, dirty water on my jeans. I turn away from Firefly Troop 423 and climb onto the bus.

Daddy settles into a seat, holding Dylan. He doesn't look at me or Mama, but I can see the muscle in his jaw working. Mama's always said Daddy may be a man of few words, but his face and hands speak volumes. When Daddy's jaw muscles work like that, it means he's worried and frustrated.

I slide into an empty seat a couple of rows back. Mama plops down next to me with a sigh. "What a day," she says.

I'm too tired to say anything. The Firefly Girls motto is "Let Your Light Shine." I don't feel very shiny right now.

Mama looks down at my wet, dirty shoes. I look down at hers. They're not in much better shape.

She shakes her head and brushes the hair away from my face. "It never crossed my mind we'd need different shoes."

"Me neither," I say. "I never knew snow would be so wet."

"Or cold," Mama adds. The corner of her mouth twitches.

"Or white!" I giggle.

"And fall straight from the sky!" Mama crows.

Don't ask me why, but me and Mama both start

laughing so hard, we can't stop.

"Who knew!" I gasp between giggles.

Mama makes her eyes big and round. "Who knew?"

Daddy looks at us like we've completely lost our minds. We probably have. He shakes his head and turns around.

Mama wipes tears off her cheeks and leans her head on my shoulder. "Oh, Piper," she says, "what in the world would I do without you?"

She takes my hand and squeezes it three times for "I love you." I squeeze back twice: "How much?" In answer, she squeezes my hand so hard I know I'll feel that squeeze even when I'm asleep.

∾ 12 ∾

Jewel

Jewel sleeps a fitful sleep on a thin blanket on top of even thinner cardboard in the doorway of a bathroom in the park where she and Baby live. In her dreams she is lost in a long hallway lined with doors, all locked. She once had a key. Where is the key? Where did she leave the key? Panic floods every inch of her body until she feels Baby's heart beating against her chest.

A car door slams. Voices drift through the cold morning air. Baby worms and wriggles out of her coat, stands on Jewel's chest, thrusts his unaccountably tall ears forward.

Jewel watches him for clues. How keen his ears, how clever his nose. Baby wags his little tail tentatively at first, then a full-bodied wag of joy. "Friends?" Jewel asks, pushing the blanket aside, standing slowly. And then she sees them coming across the parking lot. The last of the morning snow glitters all around them, halos of diamond dust.

"Angels," Jewel whispers.

Behind them, they pull wagons. "Who needs food?" one calls. "Who needs blankets?" someone else asks.

Jewel squints. She is quite sure she can see wings folded, barely concealed under their coats.

Like shadows, from under the sheltering arms of trees, picnic tables, bathroom doorways, a dumpster. The people of the park come.

Ree and Ajax.

Judy, Trooper, and Doc.

Tony and Rudy.

Linda and Duke.

Tommy and Buzz.

Jerry and Lucky.

"Our family, Baby," Jewel says. She kisses the white snowflake on the top of his head.

The angels bless each and every one with thick blankets, sheets of plastic, hats and gloves, sandwiches, oranges, apples, bananas, leashes, collars, dog food, cat food, dog jackets.

"Thank you kindly."

"Bless you."

"Bless you."

Jewel pulls a hat onto her head and down over her ears. She closes her eyes and smiles. "Warm," she whispers. "Like God's love."

The man with the barely concealed wings paws through the piles in his wagon.

"Try these," he says, holding out a pair of gloves.

Gently, Jewel puts Baby down and pulls on the gloves. "Divine," she sighs. Baby sniffs Jewel's hands and sneezes.

The man laughs and scratches the top of Baby's head.

"Where Baby and I come from, we only needed gloves for church on Sundays."

"Where did you and Baby live?"

Jewel starts to say the name of a place filled with warmth and music and yellow, but it's gone. The door won't open.

She's lost the key.

She frowns. She plucks at her hair. She picks up Baby and clutches him to her heart. "I can't remember."

Baby smells her confusion.

"Why can't I remember?"

The angel touches her shoulder, bringing her back. She blinks. Her heart slows.

"God bless you," she says.

She watches as the angels pull their empty wagons back across the park toward the parking lot, leaving narrow straight lines in the white snow, their wings barely concealed.

13

No Dogs Allowed

Baby stands next to Jewel waiting
in a line of sounds and smells.
Baby hears the shhh shhh
of restless feet
on concrete.
He smells
sharp black coffee
sweet yellow butter
earthy brown potatoes
salty white cheese
riding on warm waves of scent
from the inside
to the outside
where the line of restless feet
and cold hands

and empty stomachs
wait.
Oh, but he is hungry,
that Baby is!
All day as the sun crossed the sky,
Jewel slept.
She did not eat the bit of food
Ree and Ajax brought them.
She did not answer when Ree asked,
What can I do to help?
Baby knows what will help.
Food.
His feet tap-dance.
His tail wags.
His body wiggles.
His pink tongue licks
his black lips.
Oh, how glorious it will be
to eat! He yips.
Jewel bends down with a groan and picks the little
    dog
up
and holds him close.
Baby hears her breath rattle like the plastic they slept
    under
the night before,
wrapped up tight together.

Baby hears footsteps behind them.
A newish smell,
a getting-to-know-you smell.
Baby peers over Jewel's shoulder and sees
the girl, that girl
he has seen and smelled before
in this same line.
He likes the smell of her,
the way she looks directly into his eyes
likes she's hugging him.
"Hi," the girl says in a soft voice.
Baby lays back his ears in welcome,
ears that say, "Hey, I like you too."
Beneath Jewel's coat, he wags his body.
The girl reaches out one finger.
Baby stretches out his neck to
touch nose tip
to fingertip.
Jewel moves forward
away from the girl.
Close, so close, almost inside
the smell of food!
"Morning, Jewel," a deep voice says.
"You going to leave your dog outside
so you can come inside today?"
Baby feels Jewel shudder.
He hears her say, "Please, Rick, you know I can't."

Baby wiggles against the waves of heat
coming from Jewel's skin.
"You don't sound too good, Jewel," the man says.
"Go on over to the emergency shelter
and get out of this cold."
Baby smells fear and desperation on Jewel's breath as
    she says,
"I'd have to give up Baby to stay there, Rick."
She clutches Baby so close, his heart beats in panic.
"Baby's all I have. He's my family."
Baby feels that dark thing settle on Jewel's heart.
Baby whimpers, licks her chin.
He cannot let her go to that dark place.
He must keep her from that dark place.
He nips the bottom of her ear like he used to when
he was just a pup and she'd laugh and say,
"Oh, Baby, you are such a little pistol," and then
everything
would be fine.
Instead,
Jewel bows her head against the cold, stinging rain
that has just begun,
against the faces turned away from them as they walk
    past,
all except one face,
the face of the girl.

∽ 14 ∽

Stormy Waters

I wish I could say I was so angry, so sad that that woman and Baby got turned away again in the cold and freezing rain, that I couldn't eat a bite of supper. But I did. Before I even knew it, I'd eaten every speck of spaghetti off my plate. The garlic bread was delectable. See, Mrs. Monroe? I'm still keeping up with my vocabulary, even though I haven't been to school in months. I can't believe how much I miss school, especially learning new words. Mrs. Monroe always told us that words have power, something most kids don't have much of. I want to learn as many words as I can.

Now I'm lying (or is it laying?) here on my skinny cot half listening to Mama read *Where the Wild Things Are* to Dylan. That was the book in his special bag Miss Becky gave him when we first got here. I don't know how Mama's managed it, but she's stretched out next to him reading all about Max and his adventures. Dylan listens with his eyes half closed, his thumb in his mouth, something he's been doing lately.

"The night Max wore his wolf suit and made mischief of one kind and another . . ."

Pellets of ice tick against the high window. I think again about that woman saying she'd have to give up her little dog if she came to a shelter. Where are they now? How are they keeping warm? Does anybody care?

We may not have much in this tiny room with two cots and one small window on the world. And, of course, Daddy's not with us. But at least we're warm and dry and safe.

And together. Kind of.

That's all the woman wants too.

Mama's voice stops. I look over. Both she and Dylan are fast asleep, the book resting on Mama's chest.

I slide my backpack from under the cot. I unzip it as quietly as I can. When we had to leave Cyprus Point, Mama said all we could take were our favorite clothes—those went in one of the big suitcases—and a few things that mean the most and could fit in our backpacks. Dylan, of course, filled his little backpack with plastic superheroes and his favorite Plush Pocket Pets. She said once we got settled somewhere new, we'd get everything we needed and more. So far, that hasn't happened.

I feel my way to the bottom of my pack, past my shell identification guide, my dog-eared copy of *My Side of the Mountain*, a Band-Aid box with saved-up allowance money ($22.60), an envelope with photos of my grandma Bess (before she died) and my best friends, and past my little stuffed dog, Beans, until my fingers touch a rolled-up piece of cloth. Gently, I slide it out. My Firefly Girls sash.

I unroll the sash. The electric-blue background and yellow and white dots looks like the Milky Way.

I touch each of the pins and badges: Animal Lives, Drawing, Independence (not hard to earn when both your parents work), Cooking (my specialty is macaroni and cheese), First Aid (comes in handy when you have a little brother), Reading, and my favorite: Gourmet Brownie CEO. Mama says selling brownies is my superpower.

I remember how proud I felt every time I earned a new badge or pin. Daddy gave me three dollars whenever I earned one, and Grandma Bess gave me a dollar. The money was nice, but mostly, I just loved that feeling of being good at something. Sometimes our family was a little bit like a roller coaster, what with jobs that came and went and Dylan's asthma, and taking care of Grandma Bess before she passed, and always, always worrying about money. But these badges, they were mine. They showed what I could do. At least before Daddy and Mama lost their jobs and we found ourselves without a home.

Dylan coughs. Mama murmurs something in her sleep.

Carefully, I roll up the sash and slide it back into my pack. I climb into bed and burrow under the covers.

I blink back tears, remembering my goal of earning two more badges by the end of the year. It seemed so possible then. Now it doesn't.

Then I remember: the flyer stapled to a pole announcing a Firefly Girls meeting. What troop was it? Did it say when they would meet, and where? Hope flickers in my heart like a firefly on a summer night.

But now look where I am, who I am. How can I ever be part of a Firefly troop when I live in a homeless shelter?

∽ 15 ∽

Stay

Later, much later
Baby knows
deep in his bones
everything is wrong.
Jewel shivers and shakes
but her body is hot.
Jewel sleeps but does not rest.
Baby feels her legs twitch,
her hands reach for things not there.
Baby listens as she moans and mutters in her sleep.
Baby has heard her do this before and yet
everything was fine.
The sun came up.
Jewel awoke.
The world was new.

But the great, shuddering cough,
the dark rattle when she breathes,
these things fill Baby with worry.
Baby sniffs Jewel's breath.
It is wrong. It is bitter
rather than sweet.
Baby licks her face, paws her chest.
Nothing.
Panic fills the little dog's body.
His Jewel,
the Jewel who holds him and
whispers in his soft ears
that he is a good, good boy,
is not there.
She has gone somewhere far away
inside herself.
Baby barks and barks and barks and barks
not his usual barks that celebrate the day,
the barks that say, "Let's go!"
These are barks of fear,
yips of panic,
howls of despair.
Footsteps come. Voices say, "What's wrong?"
"Everything!" Baby barks. "Everything is wrong!"
Ree lifts the little dog from Jewel's chest.
She shakes Jewel by the shoulders.
"Wake up, Jewel," she says.

"Let's go!" Baby pleads.

Jewel doesn't.

More footsteps. More voices.

Soon

flashing lights,

a wailing into the just-beginning dawn.

Baby wails and howls too as men lift

Baby's Jewel

into the big car with flashing lights.

"Baby!" Jewel cries. "Where's my Baby?"

Baby hurls himself toward

his name.

A man kicks the little dog away.

Baby yelps in pain and frustration.

Jewel pulls herself up.

Her blue eyes lock onto the dog's,

on to his heart.

"Baby," she calls. "You stay, you hear me?"

Baby shivers with fear, lays his ears flat against his
     sleek head.

"You stay and be a good boy," Jewel says as they slide
     her into

the mouth of the big car

with the flashing lights.

"I'll be back, Baby."

Baby stays, shaking

from the effort of being a good boy even though

every muscle and nerve in his little body says
Go! Follow!
Baby stays even when
Ree and Ajax try to coax him away
from where Jewel told him to stay
even though he is hungry, so hungry!
Baby stays even as
the snow comes down and the wind blows
and the day passes from morning
to night
without Jewel.
Baby stays,
curled tight
on top of Jewel's bag, a bag that holds
her scent that has been his whole world
forever.
Ree and Ajax bring the little dog food but
hunger has passed.
Linda and Duke bring him an extra blanket but
it does not smell like Jewel and Baby together.
Instead, he curls up inside the bag with Jewel's smell,
listens to his own steadfast heart, not hers,
and waits.

❧ 16 ❧

Ree and Ajax

The weather is crazy here. For two days, it snowed and blew like a hurricane and was so cold we had to wear our hats to bed.

Today, it's sunny and so warm all the snow is gone and we've put our coats away.

"Now remember what I said," Mama says for the sixtieth time as she reties Dylan's shoes for the hundredth time, "you mind Miss Alvarez the same way you'd mind me. I don't want any reports of you disrespecting her, you hear?"

Dylan nods. Mama gently takes his thumb out of his mouth and kisses it. Which I think is gross.

Mama looks up at me. "Piper?"

"Yes, Mama," I say. I'm really glad I don't have to hang around all day in lines with Mama and

Daddy. It'll be fun to spend time with someone my own age.

Dylan asks for probably the 110th time, "You'll come back, won't you?" The thumb goes back in his mouth.

"Of course we'll come back, baby," she says. "We'll only be gone a few hours."

"But . . ."

Mama glances out the front doors of the lobby. Daddy's out front, waiting.

"Come on," Mama says, taking her purse and Dylan's hand. "We need to get going."

"You're coming, aren't you, Piper?" Dylan asks.

I ruffle his still-wet hair. "Course I am."

Gabby and her brothers, Ricky and Luke, and their mom wait for us in the lobby. Luke is just a little thing. Gabby grins and Ricky jumps up and down. Luke hides behind his mama's legs. He's at that shy age.

"Thanks again," Mama says, touching Miss Alvarez's arm. "I promise to return the favor."

Gabby's mom nods. "You better believe it. It's hard to interview for jobs when you've got kids tagging along."

Mama gives us each a quick hug and, before Dylan can pitch a royal fit, she's out the door.

"Let's go, kids," Miss Alvarez says.

We hustle out into the bright sunshine. I hear the door to the shelter lock behind us. I look back. Miss Jean waves and mouths, "See you later." We've been here six days and I still feel a little panic when I hear that door lock.

I trot along beside Gabby as we head away from the shelter. "I don't get why they make everyone leave all day," I say.

Miss Alvarez looks back at me and shakes her head. "They think if they don't, no one will go out and look for jobs. No one will try to 'improve their situation,'" she says, crooking her fingers into quotation marks. "We'll just hang around there all day and watch TV, eat bonbons, and paint our toenails."

Gabby giggles. "We paint our toenails at night."

We turn down one street and then another. A man walks past us pushing a shopping cart with a wobbly wheel. The cart is filled with all kinds of stuff: shoes, aluminum cans, a doll missing most of its hair, big sheets of plastic, and sitting right there on top of a rolled-up blanket, a big yellow and white cat. I stop and watch them make their way through the slush on the sidewalk.

Dylan skips back to me. "Did you see that, Piper? That was a cat riding in that man's shopping cart!"

"That's Jerry and his cat, Lucky," Gabby says. "They're nice."

"Oh, okay." Dylan runs to catch up with Ricky and Luke.

We stop at the traffic light, waiting for it to change. I wonder where Baby and the woman are.

Then something catches my eye: a tall, skinny man in striped pants and a bright-yellow shirt is dancing—dancing!—at the corner across the street. He twirls and dips and glides and struts. His eyes are closed but he has the biggest smile on his face. People flow past him and around him like water. Some people drop coins in a can by his feet. Car horns honk. Some people wave, others yell out things that aren't very nice. I don't think it matters to him which they do. He just keeps dancing.

I nudge Gabby and nod toward the dancing man. "Who's that?"

She shrugs. "I don't know, but he's almost always at that corner."

The light changes. I grab Dylan's hand as we cross the street heading straight toward the dancing man. "Stay by me," I say, pulling him close.

I try not to look at the man as we step onto the sidewalk. Mama always says when you're scared, it's best to look confident and like you know where you're going. I hold my head up and try my best to put purpose in my stride.

And then it's there: the park. So many trees right

in the middle of this big city!

Dylan lets go of my hand and races to catch Ricky, who's running toward the swings.

Miss Alvarez finds a picnic table close by. She sits down and takes out her phone. Luke sticks to her like a sandbur. She looks at the screen and frowns, then sighs. I feel Gabby tense up next to me.

"You girls don't wander off," Miss Alvarez says. "I have some phone calls to make."

Gabby and I walk over to the swings.

"Where do you go to school?" I ask, pushing off with the toe of my tennis shoe.

"I don't," she says. "At least not yet. My mom says she'll get me enrolled as soon as we find a permanent place." She tucks a long lock of hair behind her ear. "I miss my old school, though."

I gaze at the mountains standing so straight and white and solid far away. "Have you ever been up in those mountains?" I ask her, changing to a less sad subject.

She looks up and follows my gaze. "No," she says. "My dad always said one day we'd go up there, but we never did."

"That's too bad," I say.

Gabby shrugs. "I don't really care. They're no big deal."

I can't believe she thinks those mountains are no

big deal. "Well, I'm going up there one day," I say. "Just you watch."

This makes Gabby smile.

Dylan jumps off his swing and runs over. "I have to go to the bathroom," he says, hopping from one foot to the other. "Bad."

I sigh. Gabby points to a gray concrete building. "They're over there."

I take Dylan's hand. "Let's go."

We trot over to the bathroom and there, tucked way back in a corner by a garbage can, is a little dog curled up on top of a duffel bag.

"It's Toto!" Dylan whispers with excitement.

The dog lays his ears back and wags his stumpy tail. His brown eyes lock onto mine. I know him.

My heart breaks into a big smile. "It's Baby!" At the sound of his name, Baby wiggles all over.

"That's that woman's dog, the one we've seen at the place where we eat, remember?"

"Oh yeah," Dylan says. "That man wouldn't let her in because she had a dog." He frowns. "It wasn't fair, was it, Piper?"

Before I can answer, Dylan jumps like a piece of popcorn. "I have to pee!" he says, and races into the bathroom.

I turn back to Baby. "Hey," I say, and squat down. "Hey, you."

Slowly, I hold my hand out for him to sniff like Grandpa Bill taught me to do. "Let him read your skin first before you pet a dog you don't know," he always said. "Your smell will tell him everything he needs to know."

The little dog must have liked what he read on my skin because he licks the tips of my fingers.

I've always wanted a dog, but we never lived anywhere that allowed them.

I reach out and touch the white patch on the top of his head. It looks like a snowflake.

I feel something inside me I didn't know was frozen, melt.

His eyes are just like the color of chocolate. I swear, when he looks into my eyes, I think he knows me too.

"What are you doing?" a gravelly voice asks.

A woman stands behind me, one hand on her hip, the other resting on the big square head of a very large dog. Her hard eyes squint down at me.

I pull my hand back and stand up. "Just saying hi to this little dog." She's really tall and the dog is really big. I don't know which to be more worried about.

The woman pushes past me and kneels down. "Hey, Baby," she says in a sweet kind of voice I'd never in a million years ever expect to come out of her mouth. "I brought you some food." She reaches into her coat and pulls out a plastic bag. The little dog whimpers and wags his tail so hard it's just a blur.

The woman folds the plastic back in such a way that it makes a bowl. She places the food on top of the duffel bag. I've never seen a dog eat so fast.

She hands me an empty yogurt container and nods toward the bathroom. "Go fill this up with water for him." Before I can point out that it's a boys' bathroom, she's turned back to the dog.

I rinse out the yogurt cup. The toilet flushes. Dylan skips out. I'd forgotten all about Dylan being in here.

"You can't be in here," he says like he's the king of the world. "This is a *boys'* bathroom."

"I know that," I say. "I'm getting water for that little dog out there."

"The dog!" he squeals with excitement. I grab the back of his shirt before he can bolt out the door. "Hey!" he yelps.

"Listen, Dylan, there's a woman out there with her dog and they're both a little, well, scary."

His eyes widen. "Really?"

"Really," I say, "so I don't want you coming out until I come get you, okay?"

He frowns and sticks out his bottom lip.

I start back out the door, then stop. "I mean it, Dylan."

For once, he listens to me.

I set the cup of water down. The dog laps it up with his pink little tongue. The woman stands off to the side, smoking a cigarette. Her dog lies beside the duffel bag watching Baby drink.

"A dog can go a lot longer without food than water," the woman says through a cloud of smoke.

I don't know what to say to that, so instead I ask, "Where's the old lady he's always with?"

The woman tosses her cigarette to the ground and stubs it out with the toe of her boot. "Got really sick the other night. Burning up with fever. I called an ambulance and they took her to the hospital."

I remember the last time I saw her. I remember the man who turned her away saying, "Jewel, you don't sound too good."

"Jewel?" I say.

The woman nods. She points to the dog. "And that's Baby." The dog wags his tail at the sound of his name.

I don't know why I do it but I say, "I'm Piper."

The woman cracks a smile. "Cool name. My name is Ree, and that"—she nods toward the big dog—"is Ajax."

We watch as Baby scratches at an old blue blanket on top of the duffel bag, then curls up with a sigh.

"What about Baby?" I ask. "Who'll take care of him?"

Ree doesn't ask what I mean, like most adults would. She tosses her long dreadlocks back. "We'll all look after him," she says. "Jewel will come back for him when she gets out of the hospital."

Gabby calls my name. She's waving to me from the swings, motioning me to come back. Her mother looks like she's wanting to leave.

"I've got to go," I say, more to Baby than to Ree.

"I gotta go too," Ree says. "Gotta fly my sign."

She scratches Baby under the chin. "You stay," she says. "I'll be back soon."

I stroke Baby's head as I watch Ree stride across the park, her dreadlocks swinging back and forth across the pack on her back. Ajax trots along beside her, his tail held high, his hip bumping her leg. The farther away they get, the more they look like one being, one strange animal with four legs.

∾ 17 ∾

Baby Knows

Baby remembers this girl
from her soft smell of kindness
and her eyes that hug him and stroke him.
This girl makes Baby feel warm
even though he is cold at night now,
and alone.
Baby knows by the way the girl holds him close
and whispers in his ear
that this girl needs him.
Her hands that stroke his ears and scratch that
    special place
under his chin
tremble just the tiniest bit
with worry.
He feels sorrow beating in her heart.

Baby knows humans carry too much.
He does not understand why humans need
so much.
There is food. There is shelter. There is play!
There is love.
Baby knows the job of a dog
is to teach their human
what is important.
The happiness
of a full belly.
The joy
of playing, leaping,
running with abandon
with friends.
The richness
of a delicious smell.
The comfort
of warm sun on your belly.
And the world complete
and whole
when there is
together.
Together.

~ 18 ~

They Eat First

Today is a week and one day we've been in this shelter and it's wearing us all down. Dylan sucks his thumb all the time now. Mama's about chewed her fingernails down to the quick, and Daddy looks like he's shrinking inside of himself. He's filling out job applications like crazy, but nobody's hiring a boat mechanic here in the mountains.

The truth is, even though Daddy's always been able to fix anything, I don't know if he's going to be able to fix this.

But right now, I'm happy. It's sunny and warm and the air smells good. We're going back to the park where Baby is. Mama is watching Gabby and her brothers so Miss Alvarez can interview for jobs today. I've got some scrambled egg and toast wrapped up in a napkin for Baby.

We pass the pole with the flyer about the Firefly Girls meeting. I stop and look at it again. The meeting was last night. In the daylight I can see the girls in the photo better. They look so happy and excited, the way I always felt in my troop back home. I do a quick calculation in my head. They'll be selling gourmet brownies soon. It's my favorite time, which makes me feel pretty sad. But then, to perk myself up, I promise as soon as we're in a real home, I'll find a Firefly Girls troop to join.

We cross to the park. Dylan and Ricky whoop and holler. "Race you to the monkey bars!" Luke tries his best to keep up.

Mama smiles for the second time. I smile too. She takes my hand and squeezes it three times, our I-love-you code. It's going to be a good day.

Mama sits on a bench by the monkey bars, pushes up the sleeves on her shirt, and tips her face up to the sun. She hums a little tune under her breath.

The sun is so warm on my back, I can't imagine it ever snowing again.

"Let's go look for leaves," Gabby says.

"What for?" I ask, looking over at the bathroom. I want so much to see Baby.

"I told the librarian I'd bring her some for a craft she's doing in her story time tomorrow." Gabby holds up a plastic grocery bag.

I sigh. "Okay, but I got something I need to do first."

"Mama," I say, "me and Gabby are going to look for leaves."

"Gabby and *I*," Mama corrects. "And don't go too far. Stay where I can see you." She closes her eyes again.

I motion for Gabby to follow me over to the bathroom.

Gabby laughs. "You drank too much orange juice this morning?"

"Ha ha," I say. "You'll see."

We trot across the grass, leaves crunching under out feet. What if Baby's not there anymore? My heart speeds up and so do my feet.

"Jeez, Piper, you must be about to wet your pants," Gabby says, trying to keep up.

I skid to a stop and peer into the dark corner. My heart drops. At first I don't see him or the duffel bag. Did somebody take them or did the old woman, Jewel, come back?

And then I hear a little yip. I look behind the big garbage can and there they are: Baby and the duffel bag. My heart leaps up. The little dog pulls his lips back and smiles right back at me!

I kneel down. "Morning, Baby," I say softly. "Are you hungry?"

I take the napkin with the scrambled egg and toast out of my pocket and hold it out.

Oh so slowly, Baby leaves his bed on top of the duffel bag. He takes one step toward me and away from the bag, then another.

"Come on," I coax. "Come eat."

Baby looks back at the safety of his bed and at my hand holding the food. He holds up one dirty white paw with indecision. I know just how that feels.

"It's okay," I murmur to him the way Mama does to me when I'm sick or sad. "It's okay, Baby."

Using Mama's comfort-voice works: Baby takes one big leap and lands right in my lap. He buries his little face in the food-filled napkin and eats.

"Oh my gosh," Gabby breathes. "He's so cute!"

I'd forgotten all about Gabby.

She squats down next to me. Baby glances up at her, gives his tail a quick wag, and goes right back to eating.

"Who does he belong to?" Gabby asks.

"This homeless lady named Jewel. I think they live here in the park."

Gabby glances around. "Where is she?"

Very gently, I stroke Baby's back. His fur is wiry in places and soft in others. "This other lady, Ree, told me that Jewel got real sick and had to be taken to the hospital."

"Poor thing," Gabby says. I'm not sure if she means the dog or the woman. I feel bad for both of them.

Gabby brightens. "Hey, maybe he could come with us while we look for leaves. I bet he'd like to play with us."

But try as we might, Baby won't leave Jewel's bag. He perches on top of the old blue blanket and pins back his ears in what looks for all the world like an apology.

"Well, let's go, then," Gabby says, snapping her fingers. I've spent enough time with her now to know she does that when she's antsy. "At least he's had food."

Then I remember what Ree said. "Hang on a sec." I take the yogurt cup beside the duffel bag and fill it with clean water from the bathroom.

Baby wags his tail in thanks. "I'll be back," I promise. It's hard to leave him. Truth is, I'd rather just hang out with Baby.

Slowly, we circle around a small pond and back toward the playground, filling the bag with leaves. Gabby chatters on and on about her old house and her friends and her old school. I don't really pay much attention until I hear her say, "and so my mom says we may go live with my cousin Louisa and her family. My aunt has a new baby and could use Mama's help."

"Wait," I say, stopping. "You're moving?"

"Well, yeah, Piper," Gabby says, throwing me a sideways look. "You think we want to stay in that shelter forever?"

"But I thought you were going to live at the family shelter and we'd stay friends and maybe go to the same school, and—"

"A family shelter is still a shelter," she snaps.

My heart sinks.

I glance over toward the bathroom. That woman, Ree, and her dog, Ajax are over there.

I nod toward the bathroom building. "That's Ree. I'm going to let her know I fed Baby."

Gabby frowns. "She looks kind of scary."

"She's okay," I assure her. At least I think so.

"Hey," I say, walking up behind Ree. She's holding Baby in her lap, whispering things I can't hear.

Ree looks up at me. "Hey yourself."

Her dog, Ajax, slowly stands. He's got that old dog kind of stiffness.

"Whoa," Gabby says. "That's a really big dog." She steps behind me, which is kind of funny because she's bigger than I am.

"Is he friendly?" she asks.

"Depends," Ree says.

"On what?" Gabby asks nervously.

"On if he's hungry or not." Ree winks at me. She sets Baby down and stands.

I see Gabby taking in the woman's camo pants, orange T-shirt, black army boots, and tattoos.

"I fed him a few minutes ago," I say, nodding toward Baby, "and gave him water too."

Ree smiles. "Everybody's feeding him. He's going to get fat." She lets out a laugh that sounds more like a bark. "Baby fat, get it?"

I shrug. I kind of don't.

"What if that old lady doesn't come back?" Gabby asks.

Ree narrows her eyes at Gabby. Gabby takes a step back. I almost do too but I don't.

"That 'old lady' has a name. It's Jewel," Ree growls. "And she'll come back for Baby."

Gabby frowns. "She could be dead, you know."

Ree shifts and says nothing.

"Besides," Gabby says in a kind of know-it-all voice I haven't heard before, "she lives here in the park with that little dog. She can't take care of him." She tosses her long black hair. I have a bad feeling about what's going to come out of her mouth next. "He'd be better off with a real family."

I've seen lots of storms build out over the Gulf of Mexico. The sky gets black, then purple. The wind blows like crazy and thunder rumbles. Then the wind stops. Everything gets still and quiet. And that's when you know the storm's about to unleash its fury. That's exactly what it feels like right now.

"A real family," Ree echoes in a low voice. She takes one step closer to Gabby. She bends down and looks right into Gabby's eyes. "You think because Jewel doesn't live in a fancy house, she doesn't love Baby?"

Gabby swallows hard. "Um, well—"

"*You think*," Ree continues in her storm-building voice, "you think that because she lives here in the park, Jewel doesn't do everything she can every day to take care of Baby?"

"I only meant—"

Ree straightens up. "You see Linda and Duke over there?" she says, pointing to a woman and dog stretched out in the sun on a blanket. "And Jerry and Lucky over there?" It's the man with the shopping cart and cat, also enjoying the sunshine. She rests her hand on the top of Ajax's broad head. "And me and Ajax standing right here?"

Gabby nods and doesn't say anything this time. Smart choice.

"Our animals always, and I mean *always*, come first. They eat first. They share our blankets when it's cold. If they're sick, we get them help."

Ree's working up a good head of steam. "And do you know why that is?"

Gabby shakes her head.

"Because we love them," Ree practically shouts. "and they love us back no matter what. When they look at us, they don't see some raggedy old guy pushing a shopping cart, or an ex–drug addict, or some faceless old woman." Ree taps her chest with each word. "They see *us*."

Silence. It feels like all the oxygen has been sucked out of the air.

"What's going on here?" We all blink at the sound of Mama's voice.

Ree glares at Mama. "These your girls?"

Without missing a beat, Mama says, "Yes, ma'am, they are." She rests a hand lightly on my shoulder. Gabby moves closer to Mama's side.

Mama tilts her chin up and stands as tall as she can, which isn't saying much. "Were they bothering you?" Mama asks.

I glance over at my mother. Mama has this cute little turned-up nose that I sorely wish I had. Daddy's nickname for Mama is "Button" because her nose is as cute as a button. But when she's mad, those nostrils flare like a wild stallion's.

Ree looks away. "No, they weren't bothering me.

I was just explaining to them that people who aren't lucky enough to have a roof over their heads need their pets more than ever and do their best to take care of them."

Mama looks from Ree to Ajax. I don't think she sees Baby. Mama nods. "I can imagine that's true," she says. She squeezes my shoulder (kind of hard) and says, "Time to go, girls."

As we head back over to the playground, I take a quick look back. Ree and Ajax are watching us. I don't know why, but I raise my hand. After a second, Ree raises hers and flashes me a peace sign. Truce.

∾ 19 ∾

Each Night

Each night
Baby follows the whisper of a scent trail
left by the ambulance that took his Jewel
away.
He puts his wet, black nose to the ground
and snuffles his way through dead leaves
and wet grass,
past the others sleeping,
dreaming,
in the park.
Each night
Baby goes a little farther from the safety
of Jewel's bag.
First, to the playground
that still holds the scent of children.

The next night,
halfway across the park.
Then next,
all the way across.
He stops.
Soon, the grass will end and the sidewalk will begin.
His heart thunders in his
little chest.
Did he hear her call his name?
He turns and runs and runs across the park,
past the small field where he ran and played
with fierce joy.
Past the playground
and to the place where Jewel
is not.
She is not there.
The fourth night,
when the moon is bright and full,
one small white paw
and then another steps from the grass
onto the sidewalk.
Cars and buses race past,
their headlights slicing across
the small dog.
Baby shivers at the sight of buildings rising and
    scraping

the night sky.
He presses his nose to the sidewalk
and searches.
The scent trail he has been following
leads into a river
of traffic.
He steps off the sidewalk.
A car horn blares.
Tires screech.
Baby freezes
then yips,
turns and flies
across the grass
as fast, faster, than he has ever run before.
Back
to the dark corner,
the blue blanket,
the duffel bag that holds all
that is left of Jewel.
Two sweaters.
A skirt her favorite shade of purple.
Two books,
one she turns to for comfort,
one that makes her sad.
And tucked away in a corner
of the duffel bag,

a small leather pouch
that Jewel used to wear around her neck,
and inside that small leather pouch,
a silver key.
Baby watches the moon rise above the trees.
He remembers how Jewel loved the moon
when it was full and gold as a coin.
All night, Jewel would talk to the moon,
watch the moon and its shadows
while Baby
leaned into Jewel, and watched her.

∽ 20 ∽

Hope House

And just like that, we're moving!

Our caseworker, Mr. Ryan, called Mama yesterday while we were at the park. He said a space had come open at Hope House, a family shelter not too far away.

Mama dropped her head into her hands. "Praise the Lord," she sighed, like the entire weight of the world had been lifted.

Now we're riding in Mr. Ryan's car on our way to Hope House. We drive past the bus station where we first arrived in this city. It seems like years ago instead of a week and a half.

We stop at a red light and there, on the corner of the intersection, I see Ree and Ajax. Ree holds a cardboard sign that says "Hungry Please Help! God

Bless!" The wind is blowing so hard it about tears the sign from her hands. Mr. Ryan eyes Ree and Ajax and sighs. Kitty-corner from Ree's spot is where the dancing man usually is. He's not there today. I wonder if he's okay.

And of course, I'm worried about Baby.

I'm also thinking and thinking about Gabby. This morning, I went down to their room to tell her the good news. But when I got down there, it was empty. I asked Miss Jean if she knew where they went. For just a minute—long enough for me to imagine us doing all kinds of fun things—I thought maybe Gabby and her family had left for Hope House too. Miss Jean shook her head. "They left first thing this morning. Gone to live with some relatives, I think." It makes me sad even though Gabby had told me they were probably going to do that. She was my only friend. Human friend, that is. She didn't even say goodbye.

The light changes. We turn the corner and there it is: the park where Baby lives. I hope I'll still be able to check on him.

We pass the library. Mr. Ryan pulls his car into a driveway. "This is it," he says, unbuckling his seat belt. "Hope House."

Mama scrambles out to see our new home. Daddy unfolds from the back seat. "Come on, you two," he says to me and Dylan, holding out his hands.

The four of us stand there on the sidewalk, the Trudeau family, looking up and up at the building before us.

Dylan says what we're all thinking: "It doesn't look like a house, Mama." He sticks his thumb in his mouth.

Daddy frowns. "It looks like a motel."

"It is—or was," Mr. Ryan says. He goes around to the back of the car and opens the trunk. "It was a motel, but now it's a family shelter. Holds a lot of people, I can tell you that."

Daddy sighs.

Mama stiffens her spine and says, "It'll be fine."

Dylan takes my hand. "Emerald City?"

He eyes the tall, gray building, which, I swear, sways in the wind. "Or the Wicked Witch of the West's castle?" Dylan asks.

I scan the top of the building. "No flying monkeys." I give his hand a little squeeze. "I think we're safe. Let's go, Toto."

Okay, this is a motel. Not a sort-of motel or a motel-converted-to-apartments motel but a real motel. Two queen-sized beds, two nightstands, a tiny round table with two chairs, some drawers, a small closet, a microwave and miniature fridge, and a tiny bathroom. My heart sinks.

None of us say anything. Mr. Ryan clears his throat.

Mama snaps out of her trance of disappointment and says in a bright, brittle voice, "This is great! We have our own bathroom! And look," she says, pointing up at one corner of the room. "A television!" Sure enough, hanging precariously (I remember that vocabulary word, Mrs. Monroe) from a bracket is a small TV.

"Yay!" Dylan crows.

Mama looks with dismay at the stains on the gold bedspreads and brown carpet. Daddy eyes a large crack over the bathroom door.

"Looks like you and Dylan will be sharing a bed, Piper," Mama says.

"Yay!" Dylan yips.

Yay.

"Let me show you around Hope House," Mr. Ryan says.

We ride the elevator down, down, down five floors to the first floor. Dylan thinks it's the coolest thing ever that, to go anywhere, we have to ride an elevator.

Mr. Ryan introduces us to the man working at the

front desk, Mr. Windward. He has earrings in both ears and lots of tattoos. But he also has a smile that says he's really and truly glad we're here. "You can call me Byron," he says. "I'm here most of the time."

Mr. Ryan shows us all these different rooms: a small library, a game room with stacked boxes of puzzles and tubs of Legos. "On Thursday mornings, they have story time in here," Mr. Ryan says, "and Friday night is family film night."

He shows Mama and Daddy the Resource Room. It has all kinds of handouts on things like jobs and getting food and medical assistance. There's even a few computers. "We also hold training classes in here on filling out job applications, making résumés, interviewing, that sort of thing."

"That's wonderful, isn't it?" Mama says, taking Daddy's hand. Daddy nods.

We walk back out to the lobby. "In the morning, from six until nine, there's cereal, fruit, and juice. That's the only meal that's served here."

Darn. More squeaky green beans and goopy gravy.

"Oh, and there's no laundromat. You'll still need to go down the street for that." Mr. Ryan must notice the disappointment on Mama's face because he says, "But once a week, you'll get fresh towels and sheets."

I see kids all different ages hanging around the

lobby with their moms. "So do we have to leave every day like at the other shelter?" I ask.

Mr. Ryan shakes his head. "No, you don't have to leave. But," he says, looking at Mama and Daddy, "until you find employment, you are expected to help out here at the shelter five hours a week each. Mr. Windward—Byron—will give you a list of chores and a schedule."

"Sounds reasonable," Mama says. Daddy nods again. Like I said, my dad's a man of few words.

Mr. Ryan jingles the keys in his pocket and glances out the window. It's started to rain. "Go ahead and get settled in. We'll meet next week." He smiles at me and Dylan. "You two need to get registered for school so you can start making friends, right?"

"Yes, sir," I say. If it were up to me, I'd start school tomorrow.

Dylan frowns. "I'm too little to go to school," he says.

"Not anymore, buddy," Daddy says. He runs his hand over Dylan's head. "Time to be a big boy."

Dylan starts to put his thumb in his mouth. He stops, looks at Daddy, and instead sticks his hand in his pocket.

I guess not having a home to call our own is making us all grow up.

* * *

After supper, after we take our turns in the bathroom, after Dylan and I crawl into bed and Mama gets in between us, after she reads *Where the Wild Things Are* twice, Mama says it's time to do what we did at night back home: list three things from the day we are grateful for.

"I'll go first," Mama says. "I'm grateful we are all together again. I'm grateful for kind people like Mr. Ryan and Mr. Windward. And," she says, "I'm grateful to not sleep on the floor."

"How about you, Dyl?" Mama asks.

Dylan blinks sleepily. "Grateful for a TV. Grateful for an elevator." He closes his eyes and rubs his nose against the pillowcase. "Grateful for a nice-smelling pillow."

Mama smiles.

"Gary, you're up," she says to Daddy. Daddy stretches his long legs out on his and Mama's bed. He looks up at the ceiling. We all wait. Finally, he says, "I'm grateful for Piper, Dylan, and Meg." Mama squeezes his leg and blinks hard.

"How about you, Piper?" Mama says.

I search my mind. Truth is, so many things about Hope House didn't turn out like I'd hoped they would. I don't have my own bed, much less my own room. We don't have our own kitchen, and the TV barely works. I sigh.

"Piper," Mama says. "Are you looking at the doughnut or the hole?"

Daddy chuckles. Dylan snores.

I look around the room. Finally, I say, "I'm grateful for our own bathroom. I'm grateful I'll get to start school soon." I search my brain hard for a third thing. "I'm grateful Daddy's here," I say.

"Amen, sugar," Daddy says with a smile. "Amen to that."

❧ 21 ❧

Ree

Jewel is four days gone now and Ree worries.

Ree worries and Linda and Duke worry and Jerry and Lucky worry. And Tommy and Buzz worry. Even Rick at the Sixth Street Community Kitchen worries.

Ree has heard the word on the street that they took Jewel uptown to Saint Mark's Hospital, where people with insurance go.

Or maybe—more likely—they've taken Jewel downtown to Mercy Memorial, where people without insurance go.

Or maybe she's been discarded, or ignored, like some useless old shoe. No good to anyone except a little brown dog with a bit of a tail and a heart that loves her, a heart that is waiting, steadfast and true.

Ree picks up Baby and folds him into her coat and holds him close, next to her heart, just the way Jewel did.

Ree hates the cold. She hates the snow and the cold winds that blow across the wide, wide valley from the mountains. Usually by this time, Ree and Ajax are long gone to sunnier, warmer places. Places where she can sleep out under a blanket of stars. Places easier on an old dog's bones.

Ree sighs. Baby licks her chin.

"I will stay with you," Ree says to the little dog, her friend's anchor. "I will find her."

Ajax rubs his age-silvered face against Ree's leg. She pulls a blanket from her pack and drapes it across the dog's scarred shoulders.

Ree kneels down and presses her forehead against his. "Who would know the real word on the street?" she whispers into ears torn and scarred from his life before Ree.

Ajax wags his tail and shuffles an old-dog dance.

Ree grins. "You're right. You're always right."

∾ 22 ∾

Serendipity

"No, Gary," I hear Mama hiss from their bed. "I am sick to death of moving. We haven't stayed in one place for more than two weeks in the last four months."

I crack open one eye. It's still dark in our room. But even though I can't see them, I can feel the anger between Mama and Daddy.

I thought when we moved to the family shelter and we could all be together, everything would be better. But Mama and Daddy have started having these whisper fights almost from the first night. They think we can't hear but we can. At least I can.

Daddy grunts something.

Mama explodes. "What do you think has changed there? We have no home, no jobs, nothing to go back to."

I think about my friends and my school and my Firefly troop back home. I have lots to go back to. But nobody asked me what I thought.

"No," Mama says in that voice that says her mind is made up, "we're staying right here. The kids start school on Monday. We're going to try to make a go of it."

I put the pillow over my head. I don't want to hear any more.

When we wake up, Daddy's already gone. Mama looks frazzled.

And Dylan has wet the bed. What almost-six-year-old wets the bed?

And guess who has to strip the bed of smelly-pee sheets?

"Why do I have to take his smelly sheets off the bed?" I ask.

Dylan stands in the bathroom doorway, crying.

"Because, young lady, I have to clean up your little brother, and because I asked you to."

I can feel anger I've been holding back for months building up inside me. I ball up my fists. Even my hair feels angry.

"He's acting like a stupid little baby!" I yank one corner of the sheet off the mattress. I hear a little ripping sound.

"I'm not a baby!" Dylan wails.

"Watch your mouth, Piper," Mama warns.

I yank the whole sheet off the mattress and throw it onto the floor.

"I've been watching my mouth forever, Mama." My heart is hammering in my ears. "I never asked to leave Cyprus Point! I never asked to be living in this stupid, stupid shelter with all of us crammed into this little room and standing in line to eat."

I can't stop what comes barreling out of my mouth next. "It's all yours and Daddy's fault!"

The looks on both Mama's and Dylan's faces make me feel about as low as a piece of lint.

Mama bursts into tears. She takes Dylan into the bathroom. When they come out, he's all cleaned up and her tears are gone.

"Take your brother down to the playroom for a while, Piper," Mama says.

"But we haven't had breakfast yet," I point out.

Mama closes her eyes. I can almost hear her counting to ten in her head. "Get some breakfast and then go to the playroom."

"Can I have three doughnuts, Mama?" Dylan asks, clasping his hands in front of his chest.

I expect Mama to say no, but she doesn't. I think she's all argued out.

* * *

I watch Dylan and another little boy build a tower out of Jenga blocks. Then, carefully, they start sliding pieces out and placing them on top. The tower sways. I hold my breath, waiting for that one piece taken away to bring it all crashing down, just like when:

Mama's hours got cut at the nursing home.

The rent went up on our house.

We had to take Dylan to the emergency room when he had an asthma attack.

We helped Grandma Bess with her medical bills.

Daddy lost his job.

Another asthma attack.

Mama's hours got cut again.

Our landlord died, the bank took back the house we rented from him, and

we get kicked out.

Crash!

And here we are. Nowhere to call home.

Tears sting my eyes. I get up and walk across the room so Dylan doesn't see how upset I am.

I study the shelves crowded with board games—Monopoly, Scrabble (I'm good at that), Risk, Candy Land (Dylan's favorite), Battleship, chess (Mama's favorite).

I look up at the row of paperbacks on the top shelf, and there, pinned to the bulletin board, is a flyer for a Firefly Girls troop meeting.

Firefly Girls Troop 423 Meets This Saturday Morning, 9:00 AM, in Conference Room 4-B. All Hope House Girls and Their Parents Welcome!

My heart leaps. A Firefly troop *here*? I can't hardly believe it. And they're meeting tomorrow morning!

I read the flyer over and over until I have it memorized.

I snap my fingers. Wait, did it say they're Troop 423? That same troop I saw on the telephone pole flyer that reminded me of good things on that cold, wet day?

Chill bumps run up my arms; my scalp prickles. I remember a vocabulary word Mrs. Monroe taught us the day before I left Cyprus Point forever: serendipity. I can hear Mrs. Monroe say, "It means the unexpected coming together of different things in a lucky way." The flyer on the pole. Moving to Hope House. Having to babysit Dylan in the playroom instead of going with Mama. Finding a Firefly Girls Troop *here*, in a shelter. Serendipity!

* * *

Saturday morning. I'm so jittery with excitement I feel like I've eaten two whole bowls of Sugar Zoom! cereal.

I don't care though. In fifteen minutes and thirty-nine seconds, we're going to my first meeting of Firefly Girls Troop 423. And Mama's going too!

On the elevator ride down to the lobby, Mama hugs me to her and says for the fourth time, "Just like old times, right, Peeper?" Peeper is what Dylan used to call me when he was little and couldn't say "Piper."

I hug her back. "Sure is."

"Morning, Piper. Morning, Mrs. Trudeau." Byron is working the front desk today. I'm always glad when he's working.

Mama chirps, "We're going to the Firefly Girls meeting this morning!"

Byron smiles. "Awesome! I love Firefly brownies."

When we get to the room, we stop in the doorway. Mama straightens my Firefly sash. It feels so, so good to wear it again.

We peer in. The room's almost empty.

"Is there a meeting here this morning?" Mama asks.

A round woman with a big smile waves us in. "Sure is. You're just a little early. Most of the folks here always run a little late."

Mama frowns. She has a thing about punctuality.

The woman sticks out her hand. "I'm Shirin Bailey, proud troop leader of Firefly Girls Troop 423."

Mama smiles. "I'm Meg Trudeau and this is my daughter, Piper."

"Come on in and let's get your vest and packet, Piper," Mrs. Bailey says. "I see you already have a sash with lots of badges and pins. Good for you!"

I try on several vests while Mama and Mrs. Bailey talk about this and that.

"We got here to the city almost two weeks ago, and every day has been a challenge."

Mrs. Bailey shakes her head. "I hear you, there's nothing easy about it."

"I just never thought we'd be in this kind of situation," Mama says.

I don't want to hear them talk about how hard life in a shelter is, so I stop listening. I run my hand over and over the bright-blue vest. I put it on, then carefully drape my sash across my chest. I hear a whole bunch of voices laughing and calling back and forth.

"Sounds like they're coming," Mrs. Bailey says.

Ten girls come shuffling, bouncing, skipping into the room. There's a couple of other white girls like me, but most of them are black and Latina. Back home in Cyprus Point, there were lots of black and Latino folks—Vietnamese too. My best friend, Robin, was from El Salvador. She taught me lots of Spanish. I miss her.

But the biggest surprise that just about makes my eyes pop out of my head is the sight of a dad bringing his daughter into the room. Wait'll I tell Daddy! Except for Byron, we haven't seen many men even though this is a family shelter. Seems like it's mostly single moms and their kids.

A small girl with a big smile struts over. "Look at you in that vest," she says, grinning. "I bet in no time, your sash will be looking amazing like mine." Her sash is, in fact, pretty awesome. She has all kinds of badges and pins, more than I do.

A tall, serious-looking girl comes over and smiles a slow, quiet smile. "Hey," she says. "Glad you came." She touches a pin on my sash. "Looks like you've been busy." She puts out her hand. "I'm Karina Bailey."

Soon all the other girls, big and little, are crowded around me, introducing themselves. They're chattering a mile a minute. I don't think I'll ever catch all their names. One tiny girl who doesn't look much older than Dylan takes my hand and smiles shyly up at me. "I'm Chloe," she whispers. "Karina's my big sister. She's the real troop leader, not our mom." She looks at her big sister with pride.

"Okay, everybody," Karina calls from the front of the room. "Roll call."

In my old troop, roll call took forever because everybody was busy talking and cutting up. Plus, it was at least twice this size.

But not Troop 423. Everybody hurries to one of the chairs Mama and Mrs. Bailey set up. There's no giggling or whispering. All the girls sit up straight and proud, eyes fixed on Karina.

One by one, Karina calls their names—Angel, Alexa, Carmen, Daria, Desiree, Chloe (Chloe lets go of my hand, shoots her arm up into the air), Jessica, Luz, Phoenix, Sapphire ("You know I'm here!"), and Trina—and each one raises their hand and says, "Here!" All except Trina.

Karina frowns. "Anybody seen Trina?"

Heads shake. Shoulders shrug.

"Well," Karina says, putting down her roll-call list, "we have someone new joining our troop today."

Karina motions me to stand up. Her mother says, "Tell us a little bit about yourself, baby."

"And don't leave nothing out," Sapphire commands. Everyone laughs.

I stand up. My stomach slides down to my toes. What all do I say? Do I tell about my life before and why we're here?

I look at the roomful of girls all looking back at me with expectant eyes. In their bright-blue vests and sashes, they look like any other Firefly troop. But they're not. They'll understand my story, even without all the details.

I take a deep breath. "My name is Piper Trudeau. I'm eleven—almost twelve—and in fifth grade. I was born and raised in Louisiana but came here from Texas."

"Whew," Sapphire says. "That's a long ways away, Louisiana."

"Sure is," several of the girls agree.

"I belonged to Firefly Girls Troop Sixty-Three back home in Cyprus Point." I start to sit down, but then I add, "And I've never seen snow before or mountains."

"We got a lot of both," Carmen says.

"Thanks, Piper," Karina says. I sit back down.

"Let's stand and recite the Firefly Girls Pledge," Karina says.

We all stand. I look around for the poster with the Firefly Pledge printed in big bold letters. That's what my old troop used to recite from. There's not one here.

I gulp. It's been so long, I don't think I remember all the words.

And then, as if a choir conductor had raised his

baton, everyone places their hands over their hearts, voices strong and confident:

I promise to do my best every day
to make the world a better place,
to demonstrate kindness, compassion,
    fairness, and strength,
and to shine my light as a beacon of hope.
I promise to respect my family, myself, and
    all living things.
Together, we are brighter.
Together, we are stronger.
Together we can make a difference.

Whew! I remembered!

For the first time in months, I feel like I'm on solid ground.

Karina taps her pencil on a piece of paper. "First item on the agenda," she says, "is new badges and pins."

My mouth drops open. Not because there are new badges and pins, but because there is an agenda. These girls are serious!

Karina's mom, Mrs. Bailey, explains all about the eleven new badges that can be earned for really cool stuff like building robots and designing computer apps and websites.

"I'm going to build a robot to do my homework," Sapphire announces.

Daria raises her hand and says, "I'm going to design a computer program to help people without a home find one."

I wonder if any of the girls in my Cyprus Point troop would have thought of something like that. Probably not. They would never be able to understand how people, and even families, can end up like this.

Next, we come to my favorite subject: brownie sales! Did I mention selling gourmet brownies is my superpower?

"This year," Karina says, "the troop in our city that sells the most brownies gets to go to Camp Cloudmont this summer for free."

"Everybody in the troop?" Luz asks in disbelief.

Karina nods. "Everybody. For free."

"We've never sold the most, though," Carmen points out.

Sapphire tosses her a look. "There's a first time for everything."

"I don't want to go up in those mountains anyway," Angel says. "Too cold. Too many bugs."

For the first time in the whole meeting, everybody starts talking at once. But I don't listen. All I can hear is that beautiful word: mountains. I feel determination swell up inside me: I will sell enough brownies to go to Camp Cloudmont or my name's not Piper Elizabeth Trudeau.

At the end of the meeting, we gather in a circle.

Karina's voice rings out strong and true, "We are Firefly Girls!"

"We are Firefly Girls!" we all say.

"We are family!" she says.

"We are family!"

"We are *somebody*!" Sapphire hollers.

My heart fills with light. "We are *somebody*!"

"And we," Karina says with pure certainty, "*will* make a difference."

After the meeting's over, I ask Mama, "Can I run over to the park real quick and check on Baby?" I've told Mama all about him.

Mama's in as good a mood as I am after the meeting. She hands me her phone. "Twenty minutes, Piper, that's all. Call as soon as you get there and as soon as you leave to come back."

I can't wait to see Baby and tell him all about my new Firefly troop!

23

The Girl

Baby watches the girl walk across the park
past the swings and the empty pond
where he and Duke barked at ducks
when the weather was warm.
Yesterday, when the girl came,
her feet dragged through the dead leaves,
her head down
shoulders hunched.
But today
he can feel excitement and happiness
in her steps.
Always, she smiles for him.
Always, she has food in her pockets
to share.
He can feel her heart lift,
he can sense this burden she carries

grow lighter and lighter
as he licks the crumbs from her fingers.
Sometimes, they sit together,
her arms holding him close,
her whispers tickling his ears.
And that is enough for them both.
Other times, they run
walk
explore
play together.
And that is enough for them both.
Until Baby feels the pull of his place with Jewel
and returns to the brown bag and blue blanket
and waits.
Today
Baby watches as the girl walks across the park.
Her head lifts. Her face lights up.
She waves her arm in wide arcs
of happiness.
Baby feels the hug in her eyes.
For the first time, Baby does not wait.
He leaps from the blue blanket
and rockets
to her outstretched arms.
Oh joy!

∼ 24 ∼

The Homeless Bus

Monday. It's the first day of school for me, and kindergarten for Dylan. There's a bus that picks up all of us kids from the shelter and takes us to the different schools. Our school, Olympia Elementary, is only a few blocks away. I said I could walk, but Mama says I have to ride the bus because she's not too sure how safe the neighborhood is. So far, everybody around here seems okay to me, but I don't argue.

This is Daddy's first day too. He got temporary work at a big home improvement store. He doesn't seem real happy about it—says a monkey could do what he'll be doing—but it's honest work.

The bus pulls up and I climb on board. I slide into a seat in the back and drink in the familiar smell—chewing gum, lunchboxes, stinky socks, and gasoline—that makes up a school bus. I never thought the smell of a bus could be comforting, but it is now.

"Hi," a voice says.

I look up. It's Karina from my new Firefly troop. I'm super glad to see a familiar face.

I try to smile around my nervous stomach. "Hey," I say back.

She slides in next to me. Doesn't ask, just does it.

"Olympia Elementary?" she asks.

"Yes."

"First day?"

"Yes," I answer. "I hate starting a new school."

"Me too," she says, "but it's a pretty nice school. What grade?"

"Fifth," I reply.

"I'm in sixth," she says.

A bunch of other kids from the shelter load onto the bus. Some look like they just woke up but most of them look happy to be going to school. Not grumpy and whiny like the kids I rode the bus with back home.

That little spitfire of a girl Sapphire, from the Firefly Girls meeting, skips down the aisle, grinning. "Hey, Kar B.," she sings out. "What's the word today?"

Karina smiles. "The word for the day is 'magnanimous.'"

The word tickles the edges of my brain. I know what it means, I just can't remember.

"Magnanimous," the girl repeats. "Sounds big and important."

"It is," Karina says. "It means generous, giving."

I repeat the word to myself and make a silent promise to Mrs. Monroe I will use it in a sentence three times today.

"Take your seats," the bus driver calls. "Time to get moving."

Sapphire plops down in our seat and smooshes me up against Karina.

She grins at me and sticks out her hand. "Hi! Remember me? I'm Sapphire Creede, but everybody calls me Fire." She grabs my hand and shakes it like she's trying to wring out a wet towel.

"I'm Piper," I say. "Just Piper."

A girl across the aisle waves and says, "I'm Luz. I was at the meeting too. And this is my little brother, Marco."

A kid behind me taps me on the back. "Hey, I'm Jerome. This is my running buddy, Noah." Jerome punches Noah in the shoulder. "I'm the good-looking one, he's the smart one." Noah blushes and looks away.

Sapphire hoots with laughter. "Don't you wish!"

I smile and relax. I like how they tease each other,

just like my old friends did.

I let their voices wash over me while we make our way through the neighborhood. We pass the Sixth Street Community Kitchen. There's a long line of people waiting to get breakfast. We pass the Christian Center. We got winter boots there on Saturday. I curl my toes in my warm boots and smile. I run my hand over the bright-red-and-blue backpack I got full of school supplies. All of it donated. Some of the other kids on the bus have the same backpack. I hear Mrs. Monroe say, "Use the word in a sentence, please." The people who donated the supplies and backpacks are magnanimous.

We stop at two more shelters to pick up more kids. The bus is full now. I didn't know there were so many kids in the world without a home. I always thought homeless people were grownups. Not kids.

The bus comes to a stop in front of a school. The sign says Ridgeline Middle School.

Karina and some other kids get up. She slings her backpack onto her shoulder.

She eases past me. "See you later," she says.

My heart jumps. "Wait, why are you—" But she doesn't hear me.

I watch her on the crowded sidewalk, wondering why she got off at the middle school instead of

117

the elementary. A few other kids join her, including Jerome and Noah. They turn away from the school instead of going in it and walk in the same direction we're going.

I look at Sapphire. "Why did they get off the bus?"

She fidgets with something in her coat pocket. Finally, she says, "They don't want the kids at school to see them get off this bus."

"How come?"

"Because, 'Just Piper,' then the kids will know they live in a shelter. This," she says like she's explaining things to a two-year-old, "is the homeless bus."

I never in a million years thought of that.

Sapphire juts out her chin. "I don't care, though. Nobody messes with Fire."

Right around the corner—just a hop, skip, and a jump from the middle school—is Olympia Elementary.

For half a second I think about not getting off. I don't want kids knowing I live in a shelter.

Sapphire nudges me with a sharp elbow. "Come on, Just Piper."

I take a deep breath and line up behind her. Her shoulders are thrown back and her head is held high. The truth of it is, I wish some of that self-confidence would rub off on me.

As if reading my thoughts, she looks back at me, a

fierce light in her eyes. "Don't you let nobody tell you who you are because of where you live."

I square my shoulders and hold my head up too. I follow her down the steps and into the crowds. I hear Mama's voice say, "Act like you know where you're going." The problem is, I don't. Fire stops and says, "I'll show you where the office is. Mrs. Graham will get you all set up. She's real nice." I take a deep breath and follow Fire into my new school.

My new teacher, Mr. Koehler, waves me into the classroom. He takes the paper from Mrs. Graham, reads it over, and nods. Kids bump into me and past me getting into their seats. I can't get over how many kids are in this one classroom! As many as the whole fifth grade in my old school, I bet.

The bell rings. Mr. Koehler claps his hands. "Good morning," he calls above the clatter of voices and desks. "We have a new student joining us today."

My heart stops. What if he asks me to tell the class where I live? Where I'm from? My mouth goes dry as crackers.

"This is Piper Trudeau," he says, smiling. "Let's all make her feel welcome in our class."

Mr. Koehler touches my shoulder. "Piper, why don't you take that desk over by the window?"

I am so grateful I don't have to tell them anything

119

about who I am, I want to give Mr. Koehler a hug. You better believe he will be on my grateful list tonight.

I hurry back to the desk. I am so, so ready to be sitting in a school desk like any kid with a normal life.

I hear a snicker or two as I pass. I hear someone whisper, "Shelter kid." My face burns. I slide into my chair and look down at my desk. How did they know?

At lunchtime, I stand in line with my tray and my school lunch ticket. It's a different color than the tickets of kids in line ahead of me. I fold it up in my fist so no one can see it.

After I get my lunch, I look around for a place to sit. Never in all my years on God's green earth have I seen so many kids in one place. And it's so loud! It's like there's a million of Dylan and his friends yelling inside my head. I close my eyes.

"Hey." Someone touches my arm. I open my eyes. It's Noah, the kid from the bus this morning.

"Hey," I say.

He nods. "Yeah, I know. Come sit over here with us."

I follow him over to a table in the corner. Sitting there is Jerome, Karina, Luz, and a couple of other kids I don't know. I am so relieved to see them I almost cry.

But I don't. Instead, I sit down next to Karina.

"First few days are hard," she says. "But it gets better."

"I hope so," I say.

"We got your back," Jerome says. He leans in and says, "The secret is to just blend in."

Luz rolls her eyes. "When have you ever blended in?"

Noah and Jerome laugh, trade insults. I relax. Maybe it will get better.

But as the day goes on, it doesn't. It only gets worse.

I kick leaves off the sidewalk as I walk back to Hope House. After the day of stares and snickers and under-the-breath names I got called today at school, I decide Karina has the right idea: don't be caught dead riding the Homeless Bus. I guess I'm not as brave as Fire, even though she's younger than me.

I need to see Baby in the worst way. I need to feel like there's some good in this world. Plus, I saved him half of my cheese sandwich from lunch.

Baby yips when he sees me. He even comes running across the grass. I scoop him up. He covers my face with kisses. I hold him close and kiss the top of his head, right on that white snowflake.

"You don't care that I live in a shelter, do you, Baby boy?" I ask as we walk back over to the bathroom.

Baby lays back his ears and looks at me like he's hugging me with his eyes. All the bad stuff from the day starts to melt away.

I pull the sandwich from my pack and feed it to him one bite at a time. I smile for the first time all day. I feel like I matter, even if it's just to this little dog.

I hear dogs bark. There, sauntering across the park, is Ree and two dogs. The dogs are having a big time chasing each other through piles of red and yellow leaves.

Ree holds up one hand. "Hey," she calls.

The dogs stop their chase and look over at me.

Baby wiggles all over and pulls his lips back in a big ol' smile.

"You got a new dog?" I ask.

"Nah," she says, sitting down on the grass next to me. "I'm just watching Duke while Linda goes to the Fourth Street Clinic to get her meds."

I smile. "That's magnanimous of you."

Ree raises one pierced eyebrow. "Is that so?"

Before I can answer, she says, "Speaking of *magnanimous*, I think I know where Jewel is."

If Baby wasn't busy licking my chin, I would jump up with joy. "Where? How?"

Ree takes a piece of paper out of her back pocket and hands it to me. On the blue paper is written "Mercy Memorial, Room 102."

"Where did you get this?" I ask.

"A magnanimous friend who lives on the streets did some checking around and tracked her down. You've probably seen him," she continues. "He dances on the corner of State and Main Street sometimes."

I feel my jaw drop. "The dancing man? How in the world would he know where to find Jewel?"

Ree's eyes narrow. Not good.

"You think he's just some crazy old guy who dances on the street corner?"

I shrug.

"That man, whose name happens to be Jesse, knows everybody and everything that goes on in this pathetic excuse for a city."

I decide it'd be best to change the subject.

I read the paper again. "What do we do now?"

Ajax plops down next to Ree with a groan. She rubs his ears between her fingers. Then, like she had just now decided what to do, she says, "I'm going to have Linda watch Ajax and Jewel's stuff tomorrow so Baby and I can go check on Jewel."

I blink. "You and Baby? How will you get Baby into a hospital? I mean, she couldn't get into the Community Kitchen with him; I don't think a hospital is going to let you just waltz in with a dog."

Ree snorts. "Jewel's a lot more honest than I am. I'll sneak Baby in. It'll be easy," she says, tossing her long dreadlocks back. I look at her hair, her tattoos and pierced eyebrow. I shake my head.

"What?" she demands.

"You might want to lose the eyebrow ring," I say.

She squints at me hard.

I gulp. In just outside of five minutes, I've made Ree mad twice.

Then she looks pointedly at my bright-blue-and-red backpack. "Let me guess: Hope House."

I can feel my neck and ears turn red.

"How long?" she asks.

"Just six days," I say.

She nods. "Before that?"

I sigh. "The emergency shelter." I fiddle with the collar around Baby's neck. "Before *that* is kind of a long story."

She nods. "It usually is."

For the first time, I wonder what Ree's story is, but I decide it'd be best not to ask. Instead, I find myself telling her all about my first day at school and how the kids knew I lived in a shelter because I rode on the Homeless Bus and I had this stupid backpack, which I didn't think was stupid at first. I thought it was great.

Ree shakes her head. "There's all kinds of ways to brand a person."

I'm not exactly sure what that means.

Finally I ask, "Do you think if Jewel sees Baby she'll get well?"

Ree sighs. "I hope so. A kiss from Baby would be the best medicine, don't you think?"

I nod. "I do."

We sit there without saying anything for a while. I listen to the chatter of the squirrels. The air smells like carved pumpkins on Halloween. I know I need to get back to the shelter. Mama'll be wondering where I am. But I want to stay here with Baby.

Ree nudges my knee with hers. "Let's go over to the Christian Center and get you a different backpack. What do you say?"

I look at her scuffed boots, her rough hands. She sleeps out here in the cold every night. At least I'm inside where it's warm and dry.

I nudge her back with my knee. "I say that's awfully magnanimous of you."

25

Family

Baby listened to the beat of Ree's heart,
strong and steady and true.
He felt Ree's body rocking gently
back and forth
in time with the bus as it made its way
across the city.
Baby heard different sounds
in this part of the city when he and Ree
got off the bus.
Carefully, Ree zipped Baby deep into her coat
and whispered, "Don't make a sound."
Now Baby wrinkles his nose against the sharp smell
of the hospital.
Now Baby perks up his ears
when he hears a word,

a name:

Jewel.

He wants to yip with joy

But Ree told him not to make a sound.

He swallows that yip.

Which makes him sneeze.

He feels Ree tense.

He hears her heart stutter.

"Sorry," she says. "Must be all the chemicals in here."

He hears another human's voice say something sharp,
like a bark.

He feels a growl rumble in Ree's chest.

"Family," she says.

Then they are moving again, deep into that sharp
     smell.

Ree bends her head and whispers, "That was close."

She stops, pushes something with her hand.

She steps forward into a world of scents

that make Baby reel:

sharp, stinging smell of antiseptic

salty smell of sweat

welcome smell of food

dark, disturbing scent of sick

but underneath it all,

despite it all,

the smell Baby loves most in the world:

Jewel.
Baby squeals and wiggles and squirms
and claws his way out of Ree's coat
and before Ree can say a thing,
before Jewel can open her eyes,
Baby leaps from the darkness inside
Ree's coat
to the bright light
outside
and into
Jewel's arms.
Baby doesn't care about the tubes
and wires
and the smells on her body
that are not his Jewel.
Her arms are around him.
Her hand is stroking him.
Her voice,
the voice that has been his compass for seven years,
says over and over like a heartbeat, "Baby. Baby."
Everything is as it should be. Jewel and Baby
a pack of two.

Later,
after Ree takes Baby from Jewel and
tucks him back in her coat,

after Baby realizes that he is leaving Jewel,
not staying,
and his heart breaks,
Baby curls up deep inside the duffel bag
and shivers.
Baby can still smell Jewel's hands
on his fur.
He can still hear her voice saying over and over
"Baby, my Baby,"
like a heartbeat.
The wind rushes through the leafless trees
tossing branches in a wild way.
Snow is coming.
Baby can smell it,
can feel it.
He whimpers.
He rises from the nest of Jewel's things.
They are just things.
They are not Jewel.
They are not home.
She is his home.
He knows this now.
Without a backward glance,
Baby strikes out
away from the park,
away from Jewel's things,

away from Ree and Ajax
Linda and Duke
Jerry and Lucky.
Judy, Trooper, and Doc.
Away from the girl,
the girl who holds a corner of his heart.
But a corner is not a whole.
He pauses on the sidewalk and lifts his nose.
He sorts through rivers and threads of scent
until he finds the one he's looking for.
Without hesitation,
Baby goes in search of Jewel.

❦ 26 ❧

Gone

I can tell the minute I wake up, something's different. It feels so still outside, even though we're inside, like the world is wrapped up tight. At the same time, I can feel something happening.

I slip from the covers and tiptoe over to the big window. I push the thick curtain aside and gasp. The world is completely white! The buildings are white. The sidewalk and streets are white. You can't tell where one begins and the other ends. The benches beside the bus shelters are just lumps of white. The air and sky are white with snow coming straight down.

"It's something, isn't it?"

Daddy stands beside me, practically pressing his nose against the glass. His eyes are big with wonder.

"Had you ever seen snow before we moved here, Daddy?"

He shakes his head and touches one finger to the glass like maybe he can catch a flake on his fingertip. "Just wish it didn't have to be so dang cold for it to snow." I know just what he means.

"Maybe we'll get used to it," I whisper.

He looks down at me and smiles. "How about you and me get dressed and go down for a little breakfast."

I shiver with the thought of having Daddy all to myself. "Okay," I whisper.

On the elevator ride down, I tell Daddy all about the girls in Troop 423 and how some of them had been worse off than us before they came here. "Carmen and her mom used to ride the subway all night and stayed in the library during the day. Alexa, her mom, dad, and baby sister lived in their *car*, Daddy," I say, "for three whole months before they could get in to Hope House."

I shake my head, thinking about having to live in a car with Dylan. "We sure are lucky, aren't we, Daddy, that we didn't have to live in a car."

Daddy gives me a quick hug. "Sure are, baby."

When me and Daddy get to the breakfast room, we see Mrs. Arista. She and her teenage son live on the second floor. She's busy setting out the breakfast things. Everybody at Hope House has little and big chores to do. Our family will be setting up breakfast next Monday and Tuesday.

"Winter's here," Mrs. Arista says. She points to the TV up on the wall. "And lucky you, no school today!"

I look up at Daddy and grin. "I never thought about school being closed because of the snow. Maybe it's not so bad after all."

"Looks like we'll have a white Thanksgiving too," Mrs. Arista says, setting out the fruit bowl.

I frown. "Thanksgiving isn't for a while. It'll be gone by then, won't it?"

Mrs. Arista rubs the steam from the window and shakes her head. "Maybe not, *chica*. It's supposed to be cold for a long time."

Daddy gets his coffee and doughnut, I get juice and cereal. We sit down in the corner.

I feel sick to my stomach. I push the cereal bowl away. All the happiness of no school today drains away.

"What's wrong?" Daddy asks.

"I'm worried about the people in the park," I say.

He frowns. "What people in the park?"

"People without a home."

Daddy shrugs. "I imagine they've gone to the emergency shelter."

I shake my head, feeling even sicker. "They can't. They have pets. They're not allowed in unless they give up their dogs. Or cats."

Daddy studies me. "How do you know about these people?"

I tell him all about Ree and Ajax, Linda and Duke, Jerry and Lucky, but mostly about Baby and Jewel.

Daddy takes a sip of his coffee. "I don't like you being around these kinds of folks, Piper. You don't know what all problems they have."

I can just see Ree narrowing her eyes, hear her say, "*These kinds of folks?* Just what do you mean by that?"

"Daddy," I say, "they've just hit a rough patch, like us. The difference is they can't come into the shelter because of their animals."

"And," I push on, "Baby's all on his own. I mean, the others are looking after him too, but . . ." My voice trails off into a watery sniff. A tear plops onto the table. I quickly wipe it away with my sweatshirt sleeve.

Daddy nods. "That is a problem, especially in this storm."

"Daddy," I say, putting on my best pleading voice, "can we please, please go check on Baby? He's just a dog and he's all alone."

Daddy gets up and fills two Styrofoam cups with coffee. I watch his broad back as he snaps lids onto the cups. I hope I didn't lay it on too thick.

"Let's take these up to your mama and let her know school's canceled, then we'll go to the park."

On the elevator ride back up to our room, I rerun the movie I played in my head last night when

I couldn't get to sleep. I imagined Daddy or Mama meeting Baby and falling in love with him just like I have. I imagined them saying, "Oh, Piper, he's so sweet! You're right, he needs to come live with us, at least until Jewel gets out of the hospital." Or maybe she wouldn't come back to the park. Not that she'd die or anything really bad. But somehow, maybe Baby would become my dog, forever.

Daddy takes my hand in his as we cross to the park. The snow comes almost to the top of my boots. I can feel how cold his hand is even through my gloves. Daddy refuses to wear gloves. He says he needs to feel things in order to understand them.

I stop when we get to the edge of the park. Nothing looks familiar. The picnic benches and swings are all white. The big grassy areas where Gabby and I picked up leaves are white. My heart aches just a bit. I still miss Gabby.

"I don't see how anyone could live here," Daddy says.

I shake my head. I know the nooks and crannies where they sleep, but I don't see how they could be there now, in all this snow. Especially Baby.

I tug on Daddy's hand and point over to the bathrooms. "That's where Baby lives," I say.

As we walk through the snow, my heart pounds. What if Baby froze to death? What if he got buried in the snow? After all, he's such a little dog. How could I have not checked on him yesterday? He must think I've forgotten all about him.

I run the last few feet, calling out his name. "Baby! Baby!"

I skid to a stop. Snow is piled up against the concrete walls leading into the bathroom. The sidewalk is covered in thick snow. No paw prints. No footprints.

No Baby.

I feel sick all the way through.

Baby is gone. And so is the duffel bag.

27

Lost

Baby huddles in the sheltered doorway
of the library
watching thick curtains of snow
fall.
He followed the scent trail from the bus stop
where he and Ree had boarded the bus.
His nose had caught just enough scent on the bus ride
to create a map
from here to there.
Baby trusts his nose.
He's always trusted his nose
to find what he needs.
All dogs do.
Then the snow came,
at first just flecks in the streetlights,
then harder and thicker.

The snow covered the sidewalks and the streets
and the smells that guided him.
Baby is lost without that compass of scent.
He shivers, not from the cold and wet but
from not knowing what to do.
He leaves the shelter of the library,
steps back onto the sidewalk, and looks back
the way he came.
Baby whimpers with questions.
Should he go back to the park,
to the bag of Jewel's things,
the blue blanket,
to the girl who comes?
Should he keep searching for Jewel?
Snowflakes touch the end of his nose
like kisses.
He knows that soon
the sun will come up.
He knows soon
the storm will pass.
The birds say so.
Baby trusts birds (unlike squirrels).
He knows what he must do.
Baby settles in again
in the shelter of the library.
With a sigh, he rests his chin on his white paws
and waits.

～ 28 ～

Two Books and a Key

Daddy frowns at the yogurt cup in my hand. "This is what Baby drank out of, Daddy, I swear it is." I call out Baby's name again. Nothing.

"Maybe that woman, the one who owned him, came back and got him," Daddy says. He rubs his red hands together and blows on them to warm them up. Even though the snow has stopped and the sun is coming out, it's really cold.

I shake my head. "I don't think so," I say. I feel pretty sure Ree would have found a way to let me know.

Daddy looks back toward the street. "Well, we better get going, sugar. Your mama's going to be wondering what's taking us so long, and I got to go to work in a little while."

I feel a huge knot getting tighter and tighter in my

chest. What's happened to Baby?

Just then, I hear someone call out, "Hey! Hey, Piper!" I shield my eyes against the sun on the snow with my hand. There, coming toward us, are Ree and Ajax. Her long legs eat up the distance between us in no time. She's carrying something in her arms.

My heart lifts. It's the duffel bag.

Before she has a chance to say anything, I say, "Is Baby with you?"

Ree looks down at the duffel bag she cradles in her arms and shakes her head. "I had to move to underground parking at the library last night to keep out of the storm. I came over here to get Baby and Jewel's bag and he was gone."

"Did you go looking for him?" I ask hopefully.

Ree pulls on one of her dreadlocks. "Storm was too cold. I couldn't drag Ajax around in it."

"Holy moly," I mutter.

Ree looks at my dad like she's just now noticed him.

"Your father?" she asks.

I nod. Then I say, "Where do you think Baby went?"

Ree sighs. "If I had to guess, I'd say he's trying to find his way to Mercy Hospital, where Jewel is."

Jewel. How could I have forgotten?

"You found her yesterday?" I ask.

"*We* found her, me and Baby." Ree proceeds to tell me and Daddy about the bus ride to Mercy Memorial, and sneaking Baby into the hospital. "She's got severe pneumonia," Ree says. "If she hadn't gotten to the hospital when she did, the nurse said she would have died."

"I bet she felt better after seeing Baby, though," I say.

Ree nods. "I'm not a crier," she says, and I believe her, "but I got pretty choked up seeing those two together." She shakes her head. "Baby did *not* want to leave her."

Imagining what it must have been like for both Baby and Jewel to see each other again after a week apart gets me pretty choked up too.

"What's in there?" Daddy nods at the duffel bag in Ree's arms.

"Everything Jewel had to her name," Ree says. "Except Baby."

Daddy studies the canvas bag. I know he's thinking about the two suitcases and one duffel bag we brought with us that held everything we had to our name.

Ree shoves the duffel bag at him. "Here, you keep this safe."

Daddy takes a step back and puts his hands up. "We can't be getting involved."

Ree glares at him. "*Involved?*"

"What did you do with it when you went to the hospital before?" Daddy's got that stubborn set to his jaw. Ree raises her chin. Two bulls locking horns.

Like she's talking to a two-year-old, Ree says, "A friend kept it for me."

She tosses the bag at Daddy. He catches it. "It'll be safer with you. I can't be hauling it around while I'm looking for Baby," she says.

My heart has been so heavy, I'm surprised when it lifts. "You're going to look for Baby?"

"Of course I am," she says. "Linda volunteered to look after Ajax while I take the bus to the hospital."

Ajax looks up at Ree with pure adoration at the sound of his name.

I take the buttered toast out of my pocket I'd brought for Baby. I squat in front of the big dog. "Here you go, boy." I hand him the toast. I feel Daddy move closer to me. Ajax takes the toast as gently as if it were a baby bird. He licks my fingers in thanks.

Daddy places his hand on my shoulder. "We need to go, Piper."

Ree nods. "Look in there and see what you can find out about Jewel, if she has family or anything." She runs her hand over the top of her dog's head and bites her lower lip. "Who knows what they're going to do with her once she's over pneumonia."

And then she's gone, leaving us with a bag full of someone's life and a big load of worry in my heart.

What if Ree doesn't find Baby? And what if she does? What will happen to Baby? Even with everybody—Ree, Linda, the dancing man, the others— looking after him, how could such a little dog survive the winter?

Walking back to Hope House, I play the movie in my head again, the movie where Baby belongs to me and is my dog forever.

Later, after Daddy goes to work and Dylan is playing downstairs with a friend, Mama and I spread the stuff in Jewel's bag out over the bed.

This is what we find: two sweaters, two blouses, a purple skirt, a plastic grocery bag with underwear, bras, and socks, a hairbrush, a ziplock baggie with toothpaste, toothbrush, shampoo, and deodorant, a toy bunny missing one eye, a small leather Bible, and another leather book.

"The sum of a person's life," Mama says with a sigh. She thumbs through the leather book.

I poke around a little more. At the very bottom, tucked in a corner, is a small drawstring pouch. I pry it open, hold it upside down, and give it a shake. A silver key falls out onto the bedspread.

I hold the key up to the light. "What do you think this is to?" I ask. I can barely see something etched into the key: CWS3#25.

Something drops from the book Mama's holding. A photograph. A photograph of a smiling woman in a flowered dress, long silver hair held back in clips. The woman is sitting at a piano surrounded by kids dressed in their Sunday best.

Mama turns the photo over. Written on the back in old-fashioned handwriting are the words "Fall Recital."

"Huh," Mama says. "Must be a piano recital." She touches her finger lightly to the woman's face. "She's lovely and obviously very proud."

I look at the face again, the flowered dress, the long silver hair. Could it be?

And then I grab the photograph from Mama. "Look, Mama," I say, pointing at something small and brown sitting under the piano. "It's Baby!"

Mama frowns at the photograph. "Are you sure? Lots of people have little dogs like that."

I shake my head. "See that white patch on his forehead that looks like a snowflake and the white paws? That's Baby for sure."

Mama nods. "I think you're right. Jewel must have taught piano." Mama rubs her thumb across the photograph. "What in the world happened to you?" she asks the Jewel in the photograph. "What's your story?"

"What's in that notebook?" I ask Mama.

She blinks and looks down at the small leather book in her hand. On the inside, in a neat hand, is written *Jewel Knight*. I realize I've never known what her last name is.

Mama flips slowly through the yellowed, stained pages. "Looks like it's all kinds of things: addresses, dates, a few phone numbers." She frowns as she goes deeper inside the little book. "Then it sort of becomes a diary." She looks over at me. "This last part is hard to read. Worse than your handwriting."

I hold out my hand. "Can I see?"

She's right: the first part seems like an address book, except most of the addresses and even a lot of the phone numbers have been marked through or rubbed out. There's also notes that anyone would write: *Call Lexington Power and Light about bill; Meet June at Marston Drugstore; talk to Dr. Benson about new medication; take Baby to vet.* My heart leaps. "Look, Mama," I say, pointing, "she mentions Baby!"

I try to read the scribbly writing Mama couldn't read. It just seems like random thoughts not really connected to each other. *God is everywhere and in everyone! Why does June hate me? My mother's name was Jenny and she could never save a penny.* I turn the pages, reading more. On one page she wrote in big letters,

"The Sun is my Mother." On the next page, in handwriting so tiny I can barely make it out, she wrote "the world is killing me." I don't know why, but tears come to my eyes. It's like, in these pages, I'm seeing a person fall apart. A person who, before, could smile and sit up tall and proud; a person who touched other people.

I flip through the last few pages she'd written on. Most of it, even I can't read. All I can make out are single words—*hospital, light, sad, EUPHORIA* (I'll have to look that one up), *God, home, stars, pain, gone, WHY?*

And then, on the very last page, just two words: *Baby. World.*

I close the book. Baby is Jewel's whole world. And I'm sure she is his too.

I love that little dog. I'd do just about anything if he could be mine. But I have my family. The way I see it, Jewel needs Baby more than I do.

I look out the window. It's started to snow again.

I swallow past a big burning knot in my throat. "We have to help them, Mama."

～ 29 ～

Scent Trail

Skies clear.
Birds call back and forth,
fluffing their feathers against the cold.
Baby rises from behind the book drop and
shakes the wild night from his coat.
It is morning and,
he knows,
a new day.
He sniffs the air.
He puts his nose to the ground.
There,
just there,
the faint thread of a scent trail.
He remembers the smells of the day
he found his Jewel:

The spicy smell of a truck selling tacos.
The sweet, green smell of a shop filled with flowers.
The happy scents as they passed
children playing on a school playground.
The wet musk of a river,
a river that ran right beside the place
where he and Ree found Jewel.
Baby strikes out
following his nose,
ignoring everything else—
the bleating car horns,
the voices calling to him,
the thousand other smells—
as he goes from one scent marker to another,
truck
shop
school
until finally,
the smell of the river.
Just as snow begins to fall again,
Baby walks up to the front doors of
Mercy Memorial Hospital.
He takes one step.
The doors sweep open.
The smells rush out.
Memories of this place,

of finding Jewel,
of seeing her face,
of hearing her voice say his name
over and over,
and knowing that finally, finally
everything is as it should be,
these memories
pull him inside
as surely as
a fish on a line.
Bright lights.
Sharp smells sting Baby's nose.
Shiny floors slip under his snow-crusted paws.
Baby tries to find the scent trail
to Jewel.
Up one hall, down another.
A man pushing a mop
calls out, "Hey! What you doing here?"
Baby crouches, then hears
a ding!
He remembers that sound,
races toward it
through sliding doors
into a small room,
almost as small as the place in the park
where he and Jewel lived.

Doors close.
The room moves.
Baby whimpers.
Where is Jewel?
Doors slide open and Baby leaps out
glad to be away from the moving room.
He searches with his nose for something familiar,
for something of Jewel.
There, just there.
He remembers!
He gallops down the hall.
The scent-memory grows stronger.
Then,
"There it is!"
Voices shouting.
Hands grabbing.
Arms waving.
His heart hammers in his chest.
All the little dog wants
is to be with Jewel.
A big woman in a uniform bends over him.
slips something around his neck.
Tight. Too tight!
Baby twists and jumps and flips
like a fish caught on a line.
A blanket is thrown over his head.

Dark.
He is lifted up
into
arms that smell like dogs and fear.
Baby is carried down the hall.
He howls his heartbreak as they pass
Jewel's room.

⌁ 30 ⌁

Finding Baby

Daddy's still at work. Mama and Dylan walked over to the library for afternoon story time. I really like going to that library, but I didn't go. Right now, I have to take advantage of not being in school because of the snow and concentrate on finding Baby. I'll sure be adding snow days to my grateful list tonight.

Karina and Daria sit cross-legged on my bed. I'm praying they don't smell the pee accident Dylan had the other night.

Karina turns the silver key over and over in her hand. She holds it up to the light. "I'm pretty sure this is a locker key," she says.

She looks at the engraving on the key. "CWS three, number twenty-five," she reads out loud. "I'm not sure what CWS three stands for," she says, "but twenty-five must be the locker number."

"I wonder what's in there?" I say.

Karina shrugs. She raises one dark eyebrow. "Who knows? Maybe nothing, or maybe something that will tell us more about her."

"At least we know her last name is Knight," Daria says. "That's a big help."

Daria frowns over Jewel's small leather book. She's writing something down on a piece of paper. She grabs the end of her thick black braid and chews on it. "The addresses in the book are from all over the place—Oregon, Denver, even Saint Louis—so I can't tell where she lived before she and Baby ended up here."

Dang.

"But," she continues, holding up her pencil, "she does say that she has to call Lexington Power and Light."

"Isn't Lexington in Kentucky?" I ask.

Daria nods. "I think so, but we need to check it on the computer."

"Let's go down to the Resource Room," Karina says. "If we're lucky, one of the computers will be free."

Luck is with us. Someone is just leaving a computer when we get there.

Daria logs on. She types in the word *Lexington*.

We watch the screen. Daria worries the end of her braid while we wait, just like Mama does.

"Wow," Karina says, shaking her head. "Who knew so many places are named Lexington?"

Double dang. Then an idea flickers in my brain like a firefly. "What if you search the name of the electric company?"

Daria's fingers flash over the keyboard.

"Bingo!" she says with a grin. "Piper, you're a genius. That electric company is in Lexington, *Kentucky*."

Let me tell you, nobody has ever accused me of being a genius.

"That's a long ways away from here. Almost as far as where we came from in Louisiana," I say.

"Wonder why she came all this way?" Daria says.

"And how?" I add.

"Does she have family here or nearby?" Karina wonders aloud. "Could that be why she came here?"

"But then why would she and Baby be living in the park?" Daria says.

We stare at the computer screen like it'll magically tell us more.

It doesn't.

Just then, Karina's mom pops her head into the room. "Oh, there you are," she says. "I've been looking all over for you. The brownies have arrived. I need your help unloading the boxes."

Firefly Gourmet Brownies!

We shut down the computer and follow Mrs. Bailey out to her old, beat-up Ford Fiesta, otherwise known as Henry.

We carry box after box of Buttercrunch Blondies, Raspberry Swirls, Choco-Lots, Mocha Mint, Peanut Butter Supremes, Caramel Dreams, and my favorite, Pistachio Surprise.

Just as I'm about to pick up the last few boxes, I hear someone breathing hard behind me.

I whirl around. It's Ree and Ajax. Ree pants like she's just run a marathon.

She bends over with her hands on her knees. Ajax licks her face.

"Lordy," she mutters. "I got to give up the cigs."

Finally, she straightens up and looks at me. I shiver at the look in her eyes: fear.

"It's about Baby."

My heart drops like a rock into a deep, dark well.

Ree tells us a story, an improbable (my new vocab word) story. Somehow, someway, Baby went all the way across the city and found the hospital where Jewel is. He almost found her too, but animal control found him first and took him away.

155

"Idiots!" Ree waves her arms like windmills and paces in tight circles. Ajax whimpers. People step into the street to avoid her. I don't blame them.

"All he wanted was to find Jewel, and what do they do?" Ree demands.

Karina and Daria watch Ree, wide-eyed.

I can't answer because my heart is one big knot in my throat.

"They lock him up like a common criminal and haul him away," Ree spits. She jabs a finger in the air and says, "This is exactly why I hate people!"

"Where did they take him?" I manage to squeak.

"The so-called Humane Society," Ree says.

"The pound," Karina whispers.

My heart drops. I remember the pound in Cyprus Point. It was *not* exactly "humane."

I grab Ree's sleeve. She jerks her arm away. Ree does not like to be touched. "You're going to get Baby out, aren't you?" I ask.

Ree runs her hand across her face, then her shoulders slump. "I can't."

Now it's my turn to wave my arms. "What do you mean, you can't?"

" I can't take Ajax on the bus, Piper."

"But can't Linda look after him?"

Ree snorts. "I haven't seen Linda for a couple of

days. I don't know where she is. By the time I find her and catch a bus that goes to the east part of the city, the shelter will be closed. It closes at five."

I didn't think about that. I look at my watch: 4:15.

"But maybe—" I start.

"And even if I could somehow magically take Ajax on the bus, I *won't* take him anywhere near that place. They hate street people with dogs. If they had their way—"

And she is off on another tear.

Just then, Mrs. Bailey comes out to move her car. She stops dead in her tracks and quickly takes in the scene on the sidewalk. Her eyes narrow, her fists punch into her hips. "What's going on here?"

I take a deep breath and plunge into the story of Baby and Jewel. Toward the end of my telling, Mama and Dylan come back from the library.

Dylan waves at Ree. "Hi, lady," he says with a big smile.

"Is this about Baby?" Mama asks.

When Mama hears about Baby finding his way back to the hospital and being taken away by animal control, she shakes her head. "Lord, lord."

"What are we going to do, Mama?" I ask.

"I don't know what we can do, Piper."

"But they might kill him, Mama."

157

"No!" Dylan wails. "They can't kill Toto!"

Which starts Ajax howling and Ree cussing up a storm and Mama trying to quiet Dylan down.

"Everybody calm down!" Mrs. Bailey holds up her hands like she's trying to stop a freight train.

"Now," she says, pointing at Ree. "Did they tell you at the hospital which Humane Society they took this lady's dog to?"

Ree nods. She pulls her sleeve up and shows the inside of her arm to Mrs. Bailey. "I wrote down the address."

She nods. "Did you tell them that the dog belongs to a patient in their hospital?"

Ree shrugs. "I tried to, but, well, I got pretty upset and . . ." Her voice trails off.

Mrs. Bailey turns to Karina. "Go get my purse."

She points again at Ree. "You, you're coming with me so we can get this straightened out."

Before Ree can go into all the reasons she can't, I say, "Mrs. Bailey, I don't think that would be the best idea."

She studies Ree. "Probably not." She eyes me for a second, then says, "You know the whole story, don't you?"

I nod. "Pretty much."

She looks at Mama. "Is it okay if I take Piper with me to the animal shelter? So she can explain the situation?"

Dylan jumps up and down. "Bring Toto here! He can live with us, right, Mama?"

I look at Mama too, hoping against hope.

Both Mama and Mrs. Bailey shake their heads. "Dogs aren't allowed here, Piper," Mama says.

"But he's so little," I say. "I bet no one would even notice him. I'd share all my food with him and—"

I see Mama set her jaw. "Absolutely not. If they found out we had a dog, we'd be right back out on the streets."

I look at Mrs. Bailey with puppy-dog eyes. She sighs. "Your mother's right, Piper."

Karina comes out and hands her mother her purse.

Mrs. Bailey fishes out pen and paper. "Show me that address again." She reads the address off Ree's arm and writes it down on a piece of paper.

She snaps her purse shut. She looks at her watch. "Come on, Miss Piper," she says, opening the passenger door of Henry. "We need to go on a fact-finding mission before that animal shelter closes."

Suddenly, I remember something. "Hang on just a sec," I say, and race to our room.

We go up one street and then down another. I see Jerry and his cat, Lucky, sitting in the doorway of an empty store. Some people in fancy clothes are smiling, talking to him and stroking Lucky.

A little farther on, I see a guy I recognize from the park and his two little dogs. The dogs are bundled up in coats. He's holding a cardboard sign.

Mrs. B stops for a red light. She shakes her head and says, "I like dogs a lot too, and I guess I understand that they're all these folks have, but I just don't think I'd give up living inside with a roof over my head for one."

I think about something Linda told me the other day at the park when I was looking for Ree. I say to Mrs. B, "When people see them on the street with their dog or cat"—I want to make sure I include Lucky— "they aren't just street people, they're *real* people. Most everybody can relate to having a pet they love. Having their dog or cat helps them feel like they're important, even if it's just to their dog." I think some more on what Linda said. I want to make Mrs. B understand. "Linda says everybody needs another heartbeat on their side."

Mrs. Bailey nods. The light turns green. "You've given me something to think about, Piper."

Finally, we pull into the parking lot of East Valley Humane Society. It's not a dark little cinder-block building like the one in Cyprus Point. This one is big and has lots of windows. As soon as we get to the front door, though, I hear the howls and yelps and yips of desperate dogs. Is Baby's one of those voices?

We walk into the brightly lit lobby. It's clean but still smells a little like pee and Pine-Sol.

"What can I help you with?" a woman at the desk asks. She has blue streaks in her dark hair and a pierced nose.

"Do you have a little dog here you picked up from Mercy Memorial Hospital this morning?" Mrs. B asks.

The woman nods. "Oh yes. It's not every day you get a call that a dog is running loose inside a hospital." She frowns just a little. "Is he yours?"

"No," Mrs. B says, "but we do know who he belongs to."

"She's a patient at Mercy Memorial," I say. "He was trying to find her."

"That's sad," she says. "Can you keep him until she gets out of the hospital?"

Mrs. B and I look at each other. Then she says, "I'm afraid that's not possible."

The woman—her name tag says Tamara—studies us for just a minute too long. Does she see the frayed collar of Mrs. B's coat and the purse strap held together by duct tape? Does she see the one room I share with my little brother and mother and father? Are we

161

somehow branded as "homeless"?

Finally, she asks, "When will his owner be out of the hospital? Do you know?"

We shake our heads. "Soon," I say, hopefully.

"And when she does get out of the hospital, do they have a home?"

My stomach knots up. She knows. We shake our heads again.

Tamara sighs. "We can hold him for two weeks. After that, he'll be put up for adoption."

"But you can't," I say. "Baby is all Jewel has in the world!"

Tamara smiles. "Is that his name? Baby?" Her eyes soften. "Look, Baby will get very good care while he's here. Plenty of food and a bed to sleep in. We'll give him a bath and get him all up to date on his shots."

I guess that all sounds good, until she says, "He'll actually be better off here than living on the streets with his owner. Being homeless is no way for any dog to live."

All of a sudden, I feel like I'm channeling Ree. I don't care if this lady has figured out we live in a shelter. We're here to help Baby. I pull myself up tall and say, "Just because a person doesn't have a home to live in doesn't mean they don't love their dog or cat as much as someone who lives in a fancy house! And just because they live in the park, that doesn't mean Jewel isn't somebody. She is, and Baby needs her."

Mrs. Bailey puts her hand on my shoulder and squeezes. I can feel the blood pounding in my ears.

Tamara smooths some papers on her desk. She nods. "I understand."

She steps out from behind her desk and smiles. "Would you like to see him?"

My heart lifts up. "Yes, ma'am, I sure would."

Mrs. B and I follow Tamara down a long hall, through the cat room (so many kittens!), and through a door to the kennels. Row after row of big dogs, small dogs, some jumping up against the chain-link wire cages, others sleeping or huddled in the corner. Some look hopeful, some look like they've given up all hope of anything good ever happening again. I want every one of those dogs.

"Here we are," Tamara says, stopping next to a kennel at the end.

I peer into the dark. It takes me a second to see Baby curled up on a blanket in the corner. His food and water look untouched. He's trembling.

I kneel down and call to him softly, "Baby, come here, Baby."

He lifts his head and whimpers uncertainly.

"Come here, Baby," I call again. I put my fingers

through the wire so he can smell me. Ree says dogs remember everything through scent.

Sure enough, he comes slowly, timidly, over and sniffs my fingers. Then he wags his little bit of a tail. I just about burst into tears. "Hi, Baby," I manage to get out. "Hi, sweet boy."

"You can go in and sit with him for a minute if you want," Tamara offers.

She opens the door and I scoot in, sit cross-legged on the cold concrete floor and take him into my lap. He covers my face with kisses.

"I'll wait for you in the lobby, Piper," Mrs. B says. "Just a minute, though. We need to get back."

After Mrs. Bailey and Tamara leave, I hold Baby close and whisper in his soft little ear, "I promise I will find a way for you and Jewel to be together again." I rock him just a little and stroke his back. I can feel the knobby bones of his spine through his fur. "I don't know how I'm going to do it, Baby, but you've done so much good for me, it's the least I can do."

But how? I'm just a kid.

Baby sniffs my coat pocket and wags his stubby tail. I almost forgot! I pull out the little toy rabbit we found in Jewel's bag.

"Here you go, buddy."

Gently, he takes the little bunny and licks it over and over.

Baby wags his tail and looks at me like I can do anything. There's not one speck of doubt in that furry little face. Only trust.

～ 31 ～

Flying

Baby listens to the night sounds in this place,
unlike any other place
he has lived.
He listens to the sounds of
dogs whimpering their questions:
Why?
Where am I?
How long will it be until . . . ?"
He hears the wet slap of dogs lapping water
from metal bowls.
He hears the groan of the old dog two kennels away
as he eases his weary bones down on a blanket.
He hears the restless click of toenails on
the concrete floor
as dogs pace, pace, pace,

waiting.
Baby waits too.
He waits for the girl to come back.
She was here.
She held him.
She whispered his name.
He felt the beat of her true heart
and smelled sadness
and something else
on her.
Was it love?
Was it hope?
Baby wishes he could see the outside.
Baby has not slept inside for a long time.
He longs for the stars and moon
and smells of simple things:
grass
moldering leaves
thawed earth
and his Jewel.
That was home.
Baby leaves his bed and his bunny and
trots over to the wire door
of the cage.
The girl did not tell him to stay
like Jewel did.

She did not even tell him to be
a good, good boy.
What is a little dog to do?
Baby sniffs around the bottom of the door.
How will Jewel find him here?
Let's go! Baby barks.
He pushes his nose and then his head
underneath the door.
The space between
the bottom of the door and the concrete floor
is too small, even for Baby.
He paws at the wire, bites it,
until his paws and mouth bleed.
He looks up and up
at the latch he knows holds the door closed.
So far!
He leaps anyway, high
higher
higher
higher!
until his legs buckle beneath him.
Baby drinks from the bowl,
tags clinking against the metal.
He lies back down on the thick blanket
where his one-eyed bunny waits
and curls up into a tight little ball

of misery.

Finally, Baby sleeps.

He dreams of wings unfurling from his small back,

great wings lifting him up

and out

into the night sky studded with stars

and back to Jewel.

～ 32 ～

The Key

Monday morning. Karina, Daria, and I walk from the middle school to Olympia Elementary.

I tell them all about finding Baby at the Humane Society and what the lady, Tamara, said. "They'll adopt him out to someone else in two weeks if we can't figure out a way to get Baby and Jewel together, and then they'll never see each other again."

Daria nods. "My mother's biggest fear was that if the police or somebody found out we were living in our van, they'd take me and my baby sister away from her."

"That would have been terrible," I say. I can't imagine being taken away from Mama and Daddy.

Karina clears her throat. "We had to give up our dog to move into Hope House."

I stop in my tracks. "Really?"

She nods and looks down at her shoes. "I think that was the worst part of losing our apartment and ending up there, giving up Peaches. I miss her every day."

I squeeze her hand. "Then you know how important it is that Jewel doesn't lose Baby."

Karina nods. "We'll figure something out. I know we can."

"Me too," Daria says in her whispery voice.

Karina throws her shoulders back as we walk across the schoolyard, looking like the Karina who leads Troop 423. I can see the wheels of a plan turning behind her eyes. I think plan-making is Karina's superpower.

Just before we get to the front doors, she says, "Okay, here's what we're going to do: after my mom gets home from work, I'm going to borrow her phone and try calling some of those phone numbers in Jewel's book."

Before Karina can give her an assignment, Daria says, "I'm going to do some more research on the computer."

"Piper," she asks, "remind me what was Jewel's last name?"

"Knight."

"Right," she says, writing it down on a piece of paper.

The bell rings. "Piper, your job is to figure out what that key of Jewel's goes to," Karina says.

"Jeez, I don't know," I say, shrugging. "That's like looking for a needle in a haystack."

Karina bumps me with her hip. "You can do it. You're a Firefly Girl."

Lunchtime. I grab my food and hurry over to our table in the corner.

I only half listen to Jerome and Noah talk about tryouts for track. All morning, most of my brain space has been taken up with that mysterious key and why the heck Jewel and Baby came all the way out here from Kentucky in the first place. I remember how endless that bus ride was from Texas and how scary and confusing it was when we got out at the bus station.

I gasp. A chill runs over me. "Country-Wide bus station!"

Everybody stops talking and looks at me like I've gone crazy.

I grab Karina's arm. "CWS! The key! Country-Wide bus station!"

Karina nods. "That could be right." I can see the wheels working behind her brown eyes. "That could totally be right."

"Okay," Jerome says, "you've lost me here. What's the deal?"

Quickly, I fill them in on the story of Baby and Jewel.

"On the key it says 'CWS three, number twenty-five,'" I explain. "We figure the number twenty-five is a locker number, but we didn't know what CWS stood for. Until now."

Noah nods. "I think you're right. I know some bus stations have lockers."

"But what does the number three mean?" Luz asks.

We look at each other, brains puzzling and puzzling.

Noah gives me a shy, sideways look. "I know which station number three is."

"Really?"

He nods. "Me and my big brother came in at that station a few months ago from LA."

For a second, he doesn't say anything. Then he says, "We had to leave some stuff in a couple of lockers there until we found a place to stay, over at the Road Home shelter. It's pretty far away," he says. "In the south end of the city. We'd need to take the subway there."

I stand up. "I say we go there, see what's in that locker."

Karina blinks. "Now?"

"Well, no," I say, sitting back down. "After school."

Karina shakes her head. "I can't. I have to babysit my sister after school."

I look at Jerome. He frowns. "Tryouts for track are after school today. I really want to go."

"Noah, please say you can go." I've never ridden on a subway. The thought of it makes me kind of sick.

I catch a ghost of a smile on Noah's face. "Sure."

"Great," I say with relief. "But I'll need to stop by home first and get the locker key."

Luz's eyes gleam with excitement. "I bet she's got a million dollars stashed in that locker. Enough to buy a big house for her and Baby."

Karina laughs. "And maybe she'd let all of us live there too!"

Jerome snorts. "If she had a million dollars, why would she be living in a park in the winter?"

I know Jerome's right. I just hope like everything there's something in that locker to help Jewel. To tell us who she is.

❧ 33 ❧

Jewel

Jewel worries the threads of her blanket over and over until the edge unravels.

What was that woman's name, the one who came in like she owned the world, like she knew everything there was to know, and told Jewel where she could and couldn't live?

And so many questions!

"Where is your family?"

"When is your birthday?"

"What is your social security number?"

"How old are you?"

"What is your last known address?"

"Husband?"

"Sister?"

"Brother?"

Who are you, Jewel Knight?

Who are you?

Jewel watches the wind tear the last of the leaves from the tree outside her window. She longs to feel fresh air on her face and taste the sharpness of winter on her tongue.

She misses the sounds of birds, squirrels, the hiss of tires on the wet streets.

She misses Ree and Ajax, Jerry and Lucky, Linda and Duke.

Her family.

But most of all, every part of her aches for Baby. It is like a missing limb, an amputation, Jewel without Baby, she thinks.

Did she dream Baby was here?

Did she dream Baby covered her face with kisses and nested in her side like always?

And just yesterday morning, did she dream she heard a dog howl its heartbreak?

If she answers all those questions, where will they take her?

The only place she wants to be is together again with Baby, a pack of two.

34

Postcards

"I thought Fire was coming with us," Noah says. Noah and I are on the subway headed for Country-Wide Bus Station 3, in search of something, anything, that will help Jewel and Baby.

I fiddle with the pouch holding the key on a string around my neck.

Fire was coming with us. Like always, she was all ready to go.

But then, just as I was about to leave, she knocked on our door.

"I can't go," she said in a voice that didn't sound at all like Fire. Her eyes didn't dance like they usually do.

"How come?"

She looked down at her hands. "Mama's having one of her spells. She won't get out of bed or anything."

I didn't know what to say, so I just said, "Gosh, I'm sorry."

Fire swallowed hard. "Yeah, it's better if I stay close by her when she's like this. She needs me, you know?"

I nodded. "I'll let you know what we find out."

I look out the subway window. "Her mom's not feeling good, so she stayed with her," I say to Noah.

He doesn't ask a bunch of questions, just nods. That's one thing about shelter kids: you don't have to do a lot of explaining. We understand each other.

I bump his knee with mine. "I'm sure glad you came, though. I've never ridden on a subway train before."

Noah looks out the window at the lights flashing by. "I've ridden them too much."

"How come?"

He sighs. "After me and my brother came here, well, it took a while for us to find the Road Home shelter." He glances at me real quick. "The streets aren't exactly a safe place."

I nod.

Noah looks away. "So my brother and me rode the subway trains at night." He shrugs. "It was a safe place to be."

"What about your parents?" I ask.

Noah shifts in his seat. "I don't know my father. My mom's in jail for possession."

I'm not sure I want to know in possession of what.

It seems that's all he's going to say, but then, "My brother, Patrick, is older than me—nineteen. He came back from Saint Louis when he heard about Mom, got me out of foster care."

"He sounds like a great brother," I say.

Noah smiles. "He's bossy like most big brothers, always on me about school and homework, but yeah, he's okay."

I think about this. What would I do if I had to be the only one to take care of Dylan?

"He works two jobs and goes to school at night." He shakes his head. "He's always saying, 'I'm going to get us out of here and make something of myself. You too.'"

I remember the new vocabulary word Mr. Koehler taught us the other day. "He sounds *tenacious*," I say.

Noah laughs for the first time since I met him. The train stops and the doors whisk open. He stands. "Patrick would say stubbornness is *tenaciousness* turned upside down."

I laugh too. I'll have to remember to tell that to Mr. Koehler.

We take the stairs up from the platform to the outside.

Everything looks different here from where we live

in the city. It's mostly strip malls and gas stations and fast food restaurants.

And then I see them, closer and taller. My heart about leaps out of my chest. The mountains! We're so close now. I'll sell the most gourmet brownies, I just know it, and then . . .

Noah nudges me. "This way."

We hurry along the sidewalk up one block and then turn a corner. There we see it: a big sign that says Country-Wide Travel Bus Station.

A gust of cold wind follows us through the front door. A woman looks up from the ticket counter and frowns.

"What you kids doing here?"

"Just here to pick up our grandma's suitcase," I call to her, holding up the locker key.

"See that you give me that key before you leave," she mumbles.

Noah and I trot over to the long row of lockers. Some are tall, some are smaller. They all have numbers at the top.

I look at the number on the key. "Twenty-five," I read out loud.

Slowly, we walk along the rows. On the top row are odd numbers: 3, 7, 9; even numbers on the bottom.

The numbers get bigger: 11, 12, 14, 15. My heart

speeds up. So do my feet.

But then, there're no more lockers.

Were we wrong all along about it being a locker key? I feel sick with disappointment.

"There's more lockers over here," Noah says, waving from around a corner.

Sure enough, across from the bathrooms are two more rows of lockers.

16, 17, 20, 21, and finally, 25.

We stand in front of the closed door, just looking at it. I know we're both thinking the same thing: What will we see when we unlock it? I remember an old game show my grandma Bess used to watch where people had to guess what was behind a huge curtain. Was it a fabulous prize like a boat or new living room furniture? Or was it a goat? I would have liked the goat, actually.

"No time like the present," I say.

I take a deep breath. I slip the key into the lock and turn.

Click!

I pull open the metal door. We both lean in to look.

Crammed inside is a small black suitcase, the kind with wheels on it.

"Huh," Noah says.

"Yeah," I say. I reach in and pull out the suitcase. What's inside? More clues? More mysteries? A million dollars? Underwear?

"We'll take a look, see if there's anything worth keeping, then lock it back up."

"We can't," Noah says. "You just told that lady we're picking up the suitcase for our grandma. It'd look weird if we didn't take it with us."

"Plus, she said to return the key," Noah reminds me.

Crud. Mama always says one lie leads to another, until you're all tangled up like in a spider's web.

"Okay, you're right. We'll have to take it with us."

We wheel the suitcase back over to the ticket office. The wheels go *bu-bump, bu-bump* on the tile floor.

I smile and slide the key across the desk. "Here you go," I say as friendly and confident as I can. "We found our grandma's suitcase." I'm glad she can't see over her desk to my shaking knees.

She eyes us and the suitcase. She looks from me to Noah. Her eyebrows bunch together in a frown.

My stomach clenches up. Noah's black. I'm white. How could we have the same grandma?

"We gotta get home," Noah says, "or Mom's going to be super worried."

The woman sits up a little straighter and opens her mouth.

Before she can say anything, I grab Noah's hand and dash for the door.

"Thanks for your help," I call as we bang out the door, the suitcase *bu-bumping* behind.

We walk as fast as we can to the train station.

We find the platform for the train we'll take back and plop down on a bench.

"Whew!" I say. "I tell you what, that was close!"

Noah nods, panting. "Too close for me."

We look at each other. Noah nods. Slowly, I unzip the suitcase.

No bundles of dollar bills. No underwear (well, maybe a little), and no clues as far as I can see. What I do see are a few sweaters, a pair of nice leather shoes, a scarf smooth as water, and a couple of ziplock baggies. One has medicine bottles in it, the other has photographs. Maybe the photos will help.

I rummage around the corners and bottom to make sure I didn't miss anything.

"What's that?" Noah says, pointing at a small, thin paper bag. I pull it out. It has something in it.

Postcards. I flip through them—there must be about seven. I study each one, then hand them to Noah.

"They're all from different places," he says. One has a picture of a big, gleaming arch. It says "Greetings from Missouri!" Another has a picture of row after row of cornfields. Corncobs spell out "Iowa!"

One with a picture of beautiful smoky blue mountains catches my eye. "North Carolina Is Calling," it says. I flip it over. On the back Jewel has written, "I know you'd love these mountains, Sis. They remind me of home."

"Sis!"

I look at the backs of each of the postcards. All are written to Sis. All are addressed to the same place: Heartwell Manor, Room 23-B. All of them have stamps. And none were ever mailed.

"These are all addressed to Sis," I say. "And they all have the same address."

"Do you think that's where Jewel was going?" Noah asks.

"If Sis is her sister, I bet you anything that's where she and Baby were going. To family." A chill runs up and down my arms.

I grin. "We may not have found a million dollars, but I think we struck gold, finding Jewel's sister!"

Noah grins back. "I think you're right."

We slap two high fives. "I cannot believe we've found her sister!" I crow. "This will fix everything!"

A computer-type voice announces the next train coming in. It's the train we need to take back to our part of the city.

I put everything back into the suitcase as the train comes to a stop. Everything except the postcards. I can't believe our luck. I'm so happy, I feel like I could fly all the way back to Hope House!

The subway train rocks side to side as Noah lays the postcards out on his thighs in a line. "See," he says, pointing, "it's like they're going east to west."

He's right. The farthest-east card is the one from North Carolina.

"That would make sense," I say. "We're pretty sure she lived in Lexington, Kentucky."

Noah nods. He touches each card gently. "North Carolina. Tennessee. Arkansas, Missouri, Iowa, Nebraska." His finger comes to rest on the last one. "Colorado."

"You sure there's no more?" he asks, frowning.

I nod. "And Colorado is still a ways from here. I wonder why she stopped writing to Sis?"

The train slows. "Next stop, Library Square," the computer voice announces.

Noah gathers up the postcards and hands them to me. "Who knows. But I'd say these are the best clue you could have hoped for."

The train lurches to a stop. Noah stands. "At least if you can figure out where the heck Heartwell Manor is."

I laugh as I follow him off the train, pulling Jewel's suitcase behind.

"You might want to get you some glasses, Noah," I say. "The address is right there on the cards."

He shakes his head. "You might want to get *you* some glasses, Piper," he says.

I take the postcards out and look at the back. "Surely not," I mutter. I shuffle through them, my heart sinking with each one. They're all addressed the exact same way:

Sis
Heartwell Manor, Room 23-B

No town and no state.

~ 35 ~

Some Dogs

All day
people come and go,
come and go,
up and down the rows of
barking
jumping
tail-wagging
body-wiggling
dogs.
But not all dogs bark, jump,
wag, and wiggle.
Some dogs
look from one face to the next,
their eyes full of please,
furry vessels of barely contained
hope.

Some dogs,
not wanting to take chances
look sideways and wag
just the tip of their tail.
Some dogs
have had their hopes broken
too many times to risk
any kind of foolishness.
These dogs refuse to look
at all.
Some dogs huddle as far away from humans as they
    can,
shivering from memories of hands
hurting.
Some people say
"Too big," or
"Too old."
Some people say
"Too shy," or
"Too furry."
Some dogs leave with people
and do not come back.
Some dogs leave with people
only to come back again
smelling of disappointment.
People stop in front of Baby's cage

and smile.

"So cute!"

They kneel down and coo and cajole.

They snap their fingers and call,

"Come here! Come to me!"

Baby does not want to go to any of these people.

They are not his.

They are not his Jewel,

they are not the girl.

He turns his back, lies down with his little bunny

and licks his white paws

over and

over and over.

And waits.

∾ 36 ∾

Clues

Let's just say, Mama was not a happy camper when I got back from the bus station. And pulling what she calls a "stolen" suitcase behind me doesn't help.

"I have been *so* worried about you!" she said, throwing her hands up in the air.

"I left you a note."

Dylan whimpered. Mama turned to our bed. "You call that a note?" she said, soothing Dylan. "All it said was 'Be back soon.'"

"Yeah, but, Mama—"

Mama whirled, her eyes blazing. "Don't you 'but Mama' me. You think I don't have enough to worry about with your little brother sick and your dad working all the time?"

The doctor at the free clinic put Dylan on a new

inhaler, but his breathing still sounded like Grandma Bess's teakettle.

"I'm just trying to help Jewel and Baby," I said quietly.

Mama sank down on the bed and stroked Dylan's hair away from his face. "How about me?" she said. "I need help too, you know, especially right now."

"Yeah, but we have each other," I point out. "Baby and Jewel don't have anybody."

Somehow, I talk Mama into letting me meet up with Karina, Daria, and Fire in the computer room. "A half hour, Piper, that's all," she says. I start to argue, but when I see the mix of mad and worry on her face, I change my mind.

"Thanks, Mama," I say, giving her a quick hug.

We look over the postcards I found in Jewel's suitcase. Fire isn't her usual self, but at least she's here.

Me, I'm still buzzing with excitement about finding Jewel's sister. Well, almost.

"Noah's right," Karina says. "Jewel was going east to west when she wrote these."

"And she has family," I say. "At least a sister. That's huge!"

"It is," Daria says, "but I wonder if she wrote any more?"

Fire shrugs. "So? What does it matter?" I miss the old Fire, full of spit and vinegar. And hope.

Mr. Yee, the only dad who comes to the Firefly meetings, gets up from a computer where he's been writing a résumé.

He stretches his back.

"Can we use that computer, Mr. Yee?" Karina asks.

"Be my guest," he says, pulling out the chair.

Karina settles into the chair and logs on. "So, let's see just how many Heartwell Manors there are."

"There's probably a bunch," Fire says.

I send up a little prayer that she's wrong.

"Oh!" Daria says, pointing to the screen. "Only three!"

I glance up. Thank you!

The first one is in Georgia. "Too close to Kentucky," I say.

The next one is in Texas. "No," Daria says, "Texas is east of Colorado. That wouldn't make sense."

Karina clicks on the link to the last one. Idaho.

We look at each other with the exact same expression. I nod. "I think we might have a winner."

Karina brings up the home page of Heartwell Manor.

Daria reads out loud, "Heartwell Manor of Boise is an affordable alternative in senior living for those on a fixed income. Accommodations and amenities are based on a sliding scale."

"In other words, it's for old poor people," Fire says.

Ignoring her, Daria continues, "Along with individual suites, Heartwell Manor provides community dining, a library, a community garden, and daily enrichment activities."

"Doesn't sound too bad," I say.

"So what do we do now?" Karina asks, scrolling down the screen. "Call up and ask if they have somebody living there named Sis Knight? I seriously doubt her first name is actually Sis."

"And what if her last name's not Knight?" I know Mama's last name was Wolfe before she married Daddy and became a Trudeau. "Sis could have a married name."

"Or Knight could be Jewel's married name," Daria points out.

"Crud." I sigh. "This is getting complicated." I glance at the clock. "I have to leave in five minutes," I say. I don't want to make Mama any madder than she already is.

"Look." Karina points to a small photo at the bottom of the homepage. It shows a smiling woman holding a cat in her lap. Beneath it, it says in big letters "Pets Welcome!"

"That *has* to be where Jewel was going!" I say. "She knew she could have Baby there with her *and* be with her sister."

"Then why did she end up here, living on the streets?" Daria says.

No one answers. The clock ticks. I'm about to say I have to go when Fire says, "I think I know."

She's holding up the bag with the empty medicine bottles. She reads the names on the labels. "Lithium. Zyprexa. Klonopin." She recites the names like she knows them by heart.

She looks at us with sad eyes. "These pills are for someone with bipolar."

"What's that?" I ask.

She swallows. "It's a mental illness. My mom has it." She takes out the empty bottles and studies the labels. "These were last filled almost six months ago. Who knows how long ago she ran out."

"But she's been in the hospital," Karina points out. "Wouldn't she get her medication there?"

Fire shakes her head. "How would they know? If she hasn't been taking her pills for a long time, she probably doesn't remember she needs them."

Fire glances at us and says in a sad voice, "Sometimes, my mom doesn't think she needs her pills anymore—that she's well now—or she can't stand the side effects and she just . . . stops. Trust me," Fire says in an old, old voice, "it's *not* a good thing."

I look at the clock.

"I have to go or Mama's going to kill me." I put the postcards and pill bottles back in my pack. My fingers touch the other plastic ziplock. Photos. Dang. Too late to look at them now.

"Let's each think tonight about what we know and what to do next," Karina says like the troop leader she is. "We'll meet after school tomorrow and come up with a plan." Like I said, her superpower.

Fire and I ride the elevator up. She and her mom live on the fourth floor. For once, I'm glad this elevator is so dang slow.

"I'm sorry about your mom," I say. "That must be hard."

She nods. "I know how important those pills are because I know what my mom's like when she doesn't take them."

Fire's a head shorter than me and a year younger, but right now, she seems a lot older.

I give her a sideways hug. "You may have figured out the most important clue yet."

We reach the fourth floor. The doors slide open.

Fire raises her chin, the old glint back in her eyes. "Just call me Sherlock Holmes," she cracks.

Watching her walk off down the hall with her shoulders thrown back, I think of a word Mr. Koehler taught us: resilient. It means being able to bounce back from something really bad and move ahead. That's Fire, for sure. Now that I think about it, resilient would describe most of us kids in Hope House.

We have to be.

～ 37 ～

Questions

White coats come and go in and out of Jewel's hospital room.

The people in white coats ask more questions.

"What year is it?"

The Year of Loss.

"Who is the president of the United States?"

Jewel refuses to say his name.

"What was your mother's name before she married your father?"

What a silly question. It's her own middle name.

"Can you count to one hundred by sevens?"

Who needs to count by sevens?

Why don't they ask her something important, like, "What year did the hummingbirds come early and the dogwood bloom blood red?"

The year she was born.

"How many movements are there in Beethoven's Fifth Symphony?"

Four.

"Who wrote 'Hope is a thing with feathers'?"

Her favorite poet.

"Where is Baby?" Jewel asks.

The nurse, the kind one with eyes the color of cornflowers, says to one of the white coats, "She keeps talking about her baby."

They shake their heads.

Jewel did not know she had spoken this question out loud.

She clenches her teeth. She kicks off the covers.

Sometimes she feels like she's going to bust right out of her skin.

Sometimes she feels like she has fireworks going off in her brain.

She doesn't believe God talks to her but she thinks he should.

Then, just as soon, the Dark eats her soul.

She taps the side of her head over and over. "Things get mixed up in here."

She had been going somewhere to see someone, hadn't she? Someone important? Someone she loved?

A million lights explode in her brain.

She grabs the hand of the nurse with cornflower-blue eyes. "Sis! I have to find Sis!"

The nurse winces and tries to take her hand away.

Jewel's hands are strong from so many years of playing all four movements of Beethoven's Fifth Symphony.

Something stings her arm.

Suffocating warmth flows through her veins. Why does she feel like her body is melting?

"Please," she says one last time as her eyes close.

~ 38 ~

Anything for Jewel

We scuff through piles of leaves as we walk across the park after school. The sky is so blue it makes your eyes hurt. Except for pools of snow underneath the trees, it's hard to remember there was such a big storm just the other day.

"It sure does feel empty in the park without Baby," I say, "even though he's just a little thing."

"Good things come in small packages," Fire says with a skip. She's back to her old self, and that makes the world better.

"I know you're worried about Baby, Piper," Karina says, "but we need to focus on Jewel right now."

We sit on the picnic table near the bathroom where Baby lived.

"Here's what we know about her so far." Karina holds up one finger after another as she ticks off the facts. "One: she used to teach piano. Two: she lived in Lexington, Kentucky. Three and maybe most important, she has a sister."

"And Jewel was probably going to see her," I interrupt.

"It's also a fact Baby and Jewel need each other," I say. "And it's another fact that the shelter will put Baby up for adoption in ten days if we don't figure something out." My heart shivers like a cloud has covered up the sun.

Fire looks up. Her eyes widen. "Whoa," she says.

There, walking across the park, are Ree and Ajax. Behind them are Linda and Duke.

"Those are some big dogs." Fire scoots closer to Karina.

My heart lifts to see that tall woman with the long ropes of dreadlocks and her big ol' silver dog. I haven't seen them in days.

I wave like crazy. "Hey!" I call out. "It's me, Piper!" Which I realize is kind of a stupid thing to say.

Ree smiles her one-sided smile. She swings her pack to the ground like it's as light as a feather, which, I know for a fact, it is not.

"Hey, yourself," she says. Linda waves from behind Ree and says in a real shy voice, "Hi."

"Is that a dog or a pony?" Fire asks, pointing at Duke. A smile breaks across Linda's face. "He's a Great

Dane and my best friend. His name is Duke."

Fire shakes her head in wonder. "He better be a really good friend for all the food he probably eats. I bet he could eat two bags of dog chow a day!"

Ree laughs. "Our dogs don't want for much," she says with pride.

"Speaking of dogs," she says, "what's the word on Baby?"

We fill Ree and Linda in on what all we've found out about Baby and Jewel. Ree grabs on tight to each bit of information, keen as a hawk.

"I bet you're right about where Jewel was going," she says. "And because she ran out of her medication, she lost her way."

Linda nods. "That happens to a lot of people living on the street."

I wonder what Linda's story is.

Karina, who's been quiet since Ree showed up, finally says, "I think the two most important things right now are to let the doctors at the hospital know she needs these pills and to find out where her sister is."

Ree smiles with admiration. "I do like a girl with a plan."

"It's her superpower," I explain. "Planning, I mean."

Ree laughs from deep down in her belly.

Karina looks at her watch. "It's almost four,

probably too late to go to the hospital now."

"Maybe we can go right after school tomorrow," I say.

Fire grins. "No school tomorrow, though. It's a teacher workday."

Hope rushes through my veins. "Perfect! We can go to the hospital tomorrow. We'll take the pill bottles and postcards—and, oh, there's photographs too."

"How will we get there?" Karina asks.

"Bus," Ree says. "I'll go with you so you don't get lost."

Fire thrusts her chin up. "We're Firefly Girls. We won't get lost."

"But," Karina says, "they may not allow kids in to see patients without an adult. Hospitals have rules, you know." Karina finds comfort in rules.

Linda nods. "Ree," she says, "I'll keep Ajax while you go with the girls, okay?"

"Thanks, Linda," I say.

She smiles and tucks a strand of brown hair behind her ear. "Anything for Jewel."

"And for Baby," I say.

Daddy's working late again tonight; Mama says, not for the first time, she's about at her wit's end.

"He acts like all I do is sit around all day and night reading trashy paperback novels and painting my toenails," she says, shoving our newly cleaned clothes into drawers.

She shakes a sock at me. "Well, let me tell you," she says, the freckles on her face popping, "I'm working from sunup until sundown and after." She crams the sock into a drawer and slams it closed. "And I don't get paid!"

Dylan and I look at each other with big eyes.

Mama brushes her hair out of her eyes. She holds out her hand. "Come on, Dylan. Bath time."

While Mama gives Dylan his bath, I pull out the photographs from Jewel's suitcase and lay them out in two rows on the bed. I touch each one.

A small house with blue shutters and a big tree in the front yard.

A grainy black-and-white photo of a man with a little girl on his shoulders.

Another black-and-white photo of two girls playing with a dog.

A teenage girl sitting straight and perfect at a piano on a stage.

Two not-very-old women, arms thrown around each other, legs kicked out straight, laughing their heads off.

A tiny black and brown puppy with white paws and a white patch on his head.

I add the photo of the fall recital too.

The fall recital! Jewel had written that on the back. Maybe she'd written on the backs of the others. I flip them over, one by one.

Home
Daddy
Sis, me, and Joe
Audition
Sisters
Baby

Baby. Sis. Home. Family. All the most important things in the world.

The Wind

Baby walks on the end of a leash,
out into the warm fall sun
across dry grass and
fallen leaves,
something he has done before.
Baby walks beside someone else,
someone not Jewel,
something he has never done before.
He lifts his black, wet nose
and searches the wind,
something he has done many times.
Baby searches the wind
for answers.
Where is his home?
Where is his Jewel?

Why are they apart?
The man at the other end
of the leash
sits down on a bench,
pats Baby's small, fine head.
The hand is gentle.
It is the same hand that sets out bowls of food
every morning
up and down the rows of kennels,
always the same.
Every day, the same.
The same light,
the same smells of
Food
Water
Poop
Pee
Soap
Baby misses every day being
a new day
with his Jewel.
Baby turns his back to the man
and his hands
and the bench
and the big building filled with barking,
desperate dogs,

and sniffs.
The wind brings no answers.
He scratches at the collar around his neck.
It twists and slips up toward his ears and,
just for a moment,
Baby tries to work it over his head.
If only . . .
The man stands and
gives the leash a little tug.
"Let's go," he says.
Baby's heart leaps. His two favorite words!
He wags his tail and starts an
all-over wiggle
until
the man turns toward the building that is not
in any way
where Baby wants to go.
Baby does something he has rarely done
in his seven years on this earth:
he refuses to go.
Baby pulls back.
The collar slips a bit
toward his ears.
Baby's heart leaps with Maybe.
His body quivers with Hope!
His feet are ready to run!

The hand reaches down.
The hand scoops him up.
"Time to go back inside, little guy,"
the man says.

∽ 40 ∽

Telling About

There're five of us stuffed into Mrs. Bailey's car, Henry. Turns out she didn't have to work today because she is a teacher's aide, so we don't have to ride the bus. Karina wanted to come too, but she volunteered to watch Dylan so Mama could come instead. Given how excitable Ree can be, having Mama's negotiation superpowers might come in handy.

There was no way Fire was staying behind. She doesn't trust us to make sure the doctors know about Jewel's pills.

"Do you think they'll listen to everything we have to tell them about Jewel?" Fire asks.

I shrug *I don't know*, watching the world outside the car window. "We're just kids, and you know how adults are about that. They think we have 'overactive imaginations.'"

Fire snorts. "We don't have 'imaginations,'" she says, crooking her fingers around the word *imagination*, "we have facts."

I hope she's right.

At the front desk in the hospital, Mrs. B announces our arrival to a lady staring at her computer screen. "We are here to visit a patient, Jewel Knight."

The lady looks up from her computer and frowns. She peers past Mrs. B, taking in Ree and the rest of us. "*All* of you?" she asks.

"Yes, ma'am," I say. "We're all her friends."

"That may be," the lady says, "but only two visitors are allowed at one time."

I feel Ree tense up next to me. Ree does *not* take comfort in rules.

She takes one step forward. "She needs her friends," she growls.

"Those are the rules," the lady growls back, which is, frankly, pretty impressive.

"Ree," Mama says, "why don't you and Piper go on up and see Jewel, since she knows you. We'll stay here."

"I want to go too!" Fire stomps her foot. Sometimes I forget how young she is.

Mama cups Fire's face in her hand. "I need you to stay here with us, honey. We need to do what's best for Jewel right now."

I fiddle with the visitor's pass hanging around my neck as we ride the elevator up to the third floor. What will Jewel be like? Despite what Mama said, Jewel doesn't really know me. I talked with her that one time in line, but, well, she was kind of odd that day. I don't know if she'd remember.

On the third floor, we stop off at the nurses station to ask for directions to Jewel's room. The nurse frowns. "The patient gets easily agitated." She gives us the once-over. To Ree, she says, "You must keep your visit calm and brief." You can tell she doesn't think Ree has ever done anything calm in her life.

I touch Ree's arm and pull her away from the nurse before she can say anything back. "Yes, ma'am," I assure the nurse as we walk away. "Calm and brief."

Ree stops in front of room 102. She looks down at me, raises one eyebrow, and pushes the door open.

Jewel seems a lot smaller in the bed than I remember. Without the flowered dress, she looks all washed out.

"Hey, Jewel," Ree says softly, touching her friend's hand.

Jewel's eyes flutter open. Her gaze swims around the room until they come to rest on Ree's face. "Oh," she says. "Is it really you or am I just dreaming it's you?"

Ree smiles and squeezes her hand. "It's really me." She motions me over. "And this is my friend, Piper."

Jewel's faded blue eyes search my face. "Piper," she repeats. "What a lovely name."

"Thank you," I say. I want to tell her all about taking care of Baby and where he is now and how I promised him I'd find a way to get him back with her, and that I never break my promises, ever, but my tongue is as stiff and dry and useless as a dead fish.

"Piper helped me take care of Baby after you came to the hospital, Jewel," Ree explains. "And she's doing everything she can to help you and Baby be together again."

Jewel's eyes widen and fill with tears. "Baby!" she cries. "Where's my Baby?" She sits up taller in her bed and rakes her fingers through her silver hair. "I keep asking and asking everyone, 'Where is my Baby?' and they won't tell me. They won't tell me anything," she sobs.

Ree slips her arm around the old woman's shoulder and says in the tenderest voice, "Baby's okay, Jewel. He's in a safe place being taken care of." She shoots me a look that says, *don't say a thing.* "Now we have to make sure you'll be okay too."

My tongue gets unstuck and rises from the dead. "Miss Knight," I ask. "Were you on your way to see your sister when you, um, stopped here?"

Jewel's eyes dart around the room. "Sis? Is she here?" Before we can answer, she pushes the blankets off her legs and starts to get up. A machine beeps. "I have to find Sis!" she insists. "She's waiting for me!" The beeping gets louder.

The door to Jewel's room swings open. It's the nurse, and she doesn't look too happy.

"You need to leave," the nurse says.

"But we just got here," I protest.

"We need to calm the patient down," she says.

Ree's eyes narrow in a dangerous glare. "What are you going to do to her?" She looks like she's going to explode.

This is not going well.

"Ree," I say, pulling on Ree's arm. "Let's go. We'll come back again soon."

Ree yanks her arm away. "Don't touch me," she growls.

"You need to leave, now," the nurse says again, "or I'll call security."

"Don't leave me here," Jewel whimpers.

You can see the war inside Ree's heart in her eyes. Finally, she touches Jewel's hand. "We'll be back soon," she says. "I promise."

Ree turns and shoves past the nurse. I start to follow her out, but then I stop. I don't know what in the world gets into me—maybe Fire, maybe Mama—but I turn and say in my most dignified voice, "Her name is Jewel," I say. "Jewel Knight. She's not 'the patient,' she's a person."

Mama and Fire are working a puzzle in one of Mama's sudoku books when we get back down to the lobby. Mrs. Bailey is on her phone.

Fire jumps up when she sees us. "What happened? Did you tell the doctors about Jewel's medicine?"

My heart drops. The pill bottles. Ree, and I look at each other. How could we have forgotten?

I look away. "We didn't really have a chance to tell anyone. Things got a little, well"—I look at Mama—"tense up there. The nurse made us leave."

Ree studies her boots, frowning.

"I cannot believe y'all didn't tell that nurse about the pills!" Fire says.

"Jewel did get pretty upset and, well, confused," I say. "Maybe it was best that we left."

Mrs. B tucks her phone in her back pocket. "We'll come back next week, when I have a day off."

"Next week?" Fire explodes. "The longer she doesn't have her pills, the worse she's going to get!"

I feel tears stinging my eyes. "In a week, Baby might be adopted by someone else," I whisper.

A calm voice says, "Give me the pill bottles, honey."

Mama's holding out her hand. I press the orange bottles in her palm. She drops them in her pocket and nods toward the elevator. "Let's get this straightened out, Piper."

My heart flies up to the ceiling. If anybody can get this straightened out, my mama can.

When we get back up to the nurses station, Mama puts on her best no-nonsense smile and asks, "Who's in charge here?"

The mean nurse raises her chin. "I am."

Mama glances at her name tag. "Ms. Dillard, my daughter and I are friends of Miss Jewel Knight, a patient here." Mama takes the pill bottles out of her pocket. "And we need to talk with her doctor about medication she needs."

The nurse frowns at the orange bottles. "How do you happen to have the patient's medication?"

Mama nods at me.

I look from Mama to the nurse. "It's kind of a long story," I say.

The nurse, Ms. Dillard, crosses her arms over her chest. "I'm all ears."

I give the nurse the shortest version of Jewel and Baby's story I possibly can. Let me tell you, it's not easy.

When I'm finished, Mama turns back to Ms.

Dillard. "Could you please contact Miss Knight's doctor and explain the situation?"

The nurse's puckered mouth softens. "I had no idea about Miss Knight's situation," she says. She picks up the phone. "Her primary physician is Dr. Wells. I think she's working today."

While we wait for Dr. Wells, Mama asks, "Do you know if Miss Knight has been assigned a caseworker?" I remember some of the people at the nursing home where Mama worked had caseworkers. Some were good, some were, as Mama said, as useless as a bicycle is for a fish.

The nurse frowns. "She should have been, given her, um, living situation." She flips through Jewel's file. She shakes her head. "Doesn't look like it, though." She taps her pencil on the counter. She types something into the computer. "Let me call a friend of mine at Human Services."

Before you know it, the nurses station is filled with talking. Mama talking on the phone with Mrs. B downstairs. The nurse talking to Dr. Wells and a pretty lady named Samantha Madison. And then they're all talking to each other and across from each other, only getting bits and pieces of Jewel's story right. And none of Baby's story.

I pull on Mama's sleeve. "Jewel and Baby's story together is what's important."

Mama nods. "Excuse me, y'all," Mama says in a loud voice.

Everybody stops talking.

"If we're really going to help Jewel, you need to know the whole story."

Mama pulls me to her. "My daughter here, Piper, is the one who knows more than anybody about Miss Knight."

Dr. Wells nods. "Go on, Piper."

Oh Lord. I take a deep breath and tell them the story of Baby and Jewel.

I tell about meeting her in line at the Sixth Street Community Kitchen and falling in love with Baby. Mama's face turns a little bit pink when I say we were standing in a food line to eat. Mine does too, but I have to tell it straight.

I tell about Jewel getting sick and being taken away from Baby. I tell about Ree giving the duffel bag to Daddy for safekeeping and finding the two books and the key.

I tell about how me and my friends figured out she and Baby lived in Lexington, Kentucky, and the silver key, and the black suitcase, how the suitcase had the postcards, photographs, and medicine bottles in it.

Dr. Wells nods, looking at the labels on the bottles. "We knew Miss Knight had some, shall we say, psychological issues, but the medication we've been giving her hasn't helped. This information," she says, smiling for the first time, "will make all the difference."

Then I tell about the postcards, how Jewel was traveling across the country east to west to someone named Sis at Heartwell Manor, and how me and Karina and Daria figured out that Sis—who is Jewel's sister—lives at the Heartwell Manor in Idaho. "But we don't know what her sister's name is because it might not be Knight."

I kind of glare at the nurse. "I was going to ask Jewel about that before, but we got thrown out of her room."

I tell about Baby coming to the hospital looking for Jewel (I leave out the part about Ree sneaking him in to see Jewel before that), him ending up at East Valley Humane Society and them putting him up for adoption soon. Which would be the most terrible thing ever.

Finally, I end with, "They need each other, Baby and Jewel." And the telling is done.

No one says a word. Then Nurse Dillard says, "That's some story, Piper."

Miss Madison, who is Jewel's new caseworker, holds out her hand. "Can I see those, Piper?" I'm surprised by how reluctant I am to hand the postcards

219

and photographs over, but I do.

Miss Madison quickly flips through them and trots off for Jewel's room.

Dr. Wells gets on the phone and calls the doctor in Lexington whose name is on Jewel's medicine bottles. She nods a lot and says, "Uh-huh," and, "Yes, I see."

Dr. Wells puts her phone back in her pocket. She writes a bunch of things down on a clipboard and hands it to Nurse Dillard. "We need to start Miss Knight on these medications right away."

Miss Madison comes out of Jewel's room, smiling. She's typing something into her phone. She's got the fastest thumbs I've ever seen.

"Her sister's name is Bernadette," Miss Madison says, holding up her phone in a way that makes you wonder if this Bernadette is inside the phone, just waiting.

"She does live in Heartwell Manor in Boise, Idaho, and Jewel was, in fact, on her way to go live there too. She's been expecting Jewel for months. She's been worried sick about her."

"What happened?" I ask.

Miss Madison sighs. "I don't know for sure. I suspect she ran out of her medications early on in the trip and just, well . . ." She shrugs.

"Lost her way," I say, remembering Ree's words.

Miss Madison nods. "She's very eager, though, to

talk to Jewel. We'll do that a little later today when Jewel is a bit less confused."

Mama smiles. "That should do Jewel a world of good." She gives me a little hug. "Things are falling into place for Jewel, and it's all because of you, Piper."

Everybody—Mama, Miss Madison, Dr. Wells, even Nurse Dillard—smiles at me, nodding.

But I'm having a hard time pulling out a smile.

I'm thinking about Baby.

On the elevator ride down, I say, "We've only solved one half of the problem, Mama. We have to go over to the animal shelter and explain about Jewel and the hospital and Jewel's sister. Maybe if we explain it just right, they won't adopt Baby to someone else."

"Let's wait and see what Jewel's social worker finds out about her sister. We'll know more after that."

"But, Mama," I say, "that could take a long time, and Baby doesn't *have* a long time."

Mama sighs and pinches the bridge of her perfect nose. The elevator dings; the door slides open.

"Okay," she says, "after school tomorrow, we'll go over to the animal shelter."

I bounce on my tiptoes and clap my hands.

"But," she says, skewering me with a no-arguments look, "Dylan has to come too."

I smile up at Mama. "That's okay." There's no way I'm pushing my luck.

I take her hand and squeeze it three times.

She smiles back down at me as we walk into the sunlit lobby. She squeezes back twice for "how much?"

Ree, Fire, and Mrs. Bailey rush toward us, their questions tumbling over each other.

I squeeze Mama's hand in reply hard enough that she'll feel it and know how much, for the rest of our lives.

∽ 41 ∽

The Scent of Hope

In this place where day after day everything
is the same,
something is changing.
After food, after Outside time,
Baby is brought to a different kennel
with different smells and different light.
Here
the kennel has the sweet, milky smell
of puppies
and a female dog full of worry.
Here
the door to the lobby swings open
right by his kennel
bringing the sound of voices
and the smell of Outside.

The smell of hope.
Of going away.
All day people come and go,
looking, coaxing, whistling, calling.
Dogs are carried away in arms,
or on the end of leashes,
tails wagging,
full of hope
to new homes.
Many more dogs leave here
than in the kennel at the end
of the dark hallway.
Here the light is bright every time
the door opens.
By the end of the day
Baby is exhausted by all the new,
all the coming and going.
He rests his chin on his brown bunny
and listens to the wind
scrape across the roof above.
He misses the feel of wind and cold and
the sun on his belly.
He misses seeing the sun rise,
all the curious things of the day,
no two days the same.
Every day a new day.

Every day a good day
with Jewel.
Only with Jewel.

ᦓ 42 ᦓ

Light

Jewel lets the voice as familiar as her own run over her and through her like water on fire-scorched earth.

With every word, she feels a key open long-forgotten parts of herself.

"I have missed you so," the voice of her sister says. "Come here and stay with me."

"Come here," the voice says, "and we will grow old together."

Light appears through the dark crack and touches a memory in Jewel's soul: a poem she once loved, she once knew by heart.

She smiles and says, "Grow old along with me, the best is yet to be."

Light pours in through the crack, shining bits and pieces of the poem on Jewel.

～ 43 ～

Good News, Bad News

Can I just say I hate it when someone says, "I have good news and bad news, which one do you want first?"

That's what Mama says as we're riding the bus to the East Valley Humane Society.

I sigh. "Good news, I guess."

"Jewel talked with her sister on the phone this morning, and it went well. Jewel was very happy to hear from her and wants to go to Heartwell Manor and live there."

"That is good news," I agree. "But what's the bad news?"

"The bad news is, Jewel's sister can't come get Jewel and Baby like we were hoping."

My heart drops like a too-fast elevator. "Why not?"

"She's in a wheelchair," Mama explains.

My heart drops two stories down the Elevator of Disappointment.

"I called Country-Wide to see what a one-way ticket would cost for Jewel to get out to Idaho."

"And?"

"Well, it's not *too* bad," she says.

My heart lifts just a little.

"But," Mama continues, "they don't allow dogs on the bus."

My heart drops down, down, down. I'm getting real tired of elevators.

The shelter is quiet when we get there. The dogs must be taking naps. The same lady, Tamara, looks up from her desk when we walk in.

"Hi," she says with a smile. "What can I help you with?"

I swallow hard. "Baby," is all I manage to get out.

"Toto," Dylan says helpfully.

Recognition lights Tamara's face. "Now I remember you," she says, pointing to me. "You came in last week and told me about Baby and his person. Opal, was it? Ruby?"

"Jewel," I correct her. "Jewel Knight."

She nods. "I have to tell you, we've had a lot of interest in that little dog. I have a whole stack of applications people have filled out to adopt him."

I feel the blood rush to my face. "But you said you wouldn't put him up for adoption for two weeks."

"I know," Tamara says, "and that two weeks will be up in four days."

"But you can't!" I cry.

Mama puts her hand on my shoulder and squeezes. Then she explains everything that's happened.

Tamara taps her fingers on her desk. I can tell she's thinking things over by the way she puckers her mouth.

"So Jewel is definitely going to this place where her sister lives, and you know for sure they allow pets?"

"Yes, ma'am," Mama says. She doesn't mention that Jewel doesn't have the money for her bus ticket and neither does her sister.

"It's just that they don't allow dogs on the Country-Wide bus," I say.

"That's not fair," Dylan says, clutching Ted the Shark to his chest. "Dogs are people too."

Tamara laughs, but in a nice way. Then she says, "I have an idea that might get us around that."

She opens a folder. "Let me make some phone calls while you go visit Baby."

After supper, I meet Karina, Fire, and Daria down in the computer room. I fill them in on our visit to the animal shelter.

"Tamara says that if Baby is registered as Jewel's emotional support animal, he can ride on the bus with her," I say.

"An emotional support animal," Karina says, trying out the words. "I've never heard of that."

"It's kind of like a therapy dog," I explain. "They can go in lots of places that regular animals aren't allowed, like the post office, grocery stores, restaurants, that sort of thing."

"How does he get registered?" Daria asks.

"Jewel's doctor has to write a letter saying Jewel needs Baby to be"—I search my brain for the words Tamara used—"mentally and emotionally stable."

"That sure is the truth," Fire says.

"And that Jewel is disabled," I add, "because of her mental illness."

Fire nods. "My mom is on disability for her spells too."

"The good thing," I say, "is Jewel has a caseworker now, and she's working on all of this."

"But can this all happen in just a few days?" Daria asks.

I nod. "I think so. Tamara said she'd talk it over with her supervisor, but she thinks they can hold Baby for at least another week. The shelter also has a dog trainer who can teach Baby the things he'll need to go in public places and live in Heartwell Manor." I don't tell them, though, that Baby's been moved to a kennel near the front where the "highly adoptable" dogs are.

Daria turns from the computer screen. "It'd be great if we could get Baby one of these official vests too." Sure enough, there on the screen, is a dog wearing a red and black vest with an official-looking patch on the side. "Then everybody would know how important he is."

"How much does it cost?" Karina-the-practical asks.

"Looks like a small one is about thirty dollars," Daria says.

Fire sighs. "More money Jewel doesn't have."

I remember the leftover allowance money in my Band-Aid box. "I've got twenty dollars I can donate toward the vest for Baby."

"That's magnanimous of you, right, Karina?" Fire says with a wink.

Karina laughs. Then she says, "No kidding, but that doesn't solve the problem of the money we'll need for the bus ticket."

I take a deep breath. "I've been giving that a lot of thought," I say, "and I think I have a plan."

❧ 44 ❧

Sit! Stay!

A man with the smell of
other dogs
and chicken bits
takes Baby out into the fenced yard,
away from the barking, yipping,
and howling.
He asks Baby, "Do you know sit?"
Baby lies down.
The man asks, "Do you know down?"
Baby rolls onto his back
for a belly rub.
"I'll take that as a no," the man sighs.
The man holds his hand up, palm out, and says,
"Stay, Baby!"
He walks away.
Baby follows

the smell of chicken bits drifting
from the man's pocket.
How can he not, even though he knows that word?
The man smiles. He sits on the ground and
gathers Baby into his strong arms.
He nuzzles Baby's ears.
"We've got a lot of work to do to get you ready
to be a good doggy citizen."
Baby wags his bit of a tail.
The man gives him a tasty bite of chicken.
"You've got to learn sit, down, no, and
stay."
Baby wags his tail again, licks his lips, and sneezes
with excitement.
The man laughs and gives him another piece of
    chicken.
"When we're done, you're going to be the best
support dog there ever was."
The man stands and brushes the dirt
from his jeans.
He pats Baby on the head.
"Let's go," he says.
Finally, his favorite words.
"Let's go!" Baby yips.

45

The Power of Brownies

It's Troop 423 Firefly Girls Gourmet Brownie night. Normally, we meet on Saturday mornings, but we're meeting early so we can get going on selling brownies.

In my old troop, we sold boxes of brownies to people we knew or our parents worked with, or at church. We even sold them at school. Teachers purely love gourmet brownies.

But here, it's different. The people in Hope House don't exactly have spare money for ordering tons of brownies. Lots of the parents don't have jobs, so that's out.

"We set up tables in front of businesses that will allow us," Karina explained, walking home from school today. "Sometimes we ask our teachers too."

She shrugged. "Honestly, we don't raise lots of money."

"What do y'all do with what you do raise?"

"Oh," she said, watching two squirrels chase each other across the playground, "we usually just have enough for, like, a big pizza party or something. Sometimes enough for all of us to go to a movie."

All these weeks I've been dreaming about selling enough brownies to go to the camp up in the mountains this summer. I imagined what camp in the mountains would be like every day when I looked west.

But tonight, I have a different idea.

After roll call, we say the Firefly Pledge.

"I promise to do my best every day to make the world a better place . . ."

Tonight, those words have extra meaning for me.

Karina stands at the podium and goes through the agenda. She looks at me and says, "Piper has requested time to talk about our brownie sales." She motions for me to come up to the front.

I see Mama's face in the back of the room. She smiles and nods. "Just tell their story," I hear her say in my head.

"There's a woman named Jewel. She lives over in the park across the road with her little dog, Baby. Jewel and Baby can't be in a shelter like us where it's safe and warm because they don't allow pets in shelters. So," I say, "they have to live outside, even in the winter."

I see Alexa, Desiree, Chloe, Luz, Phoenix, and even Carmen frown.

Angel shakes her head. "That is *so* not fair."

I take a deep breath and continue their story. "Because of that, Jewel got really sick with pneumonia and is in the hospital. Baby was left alone, and he's just a little dog, kind of like Toto from *The Wizard of Oz*." Seeing how upset people look, I rush to add, "But a lot of other people who live in the park helped look after him."

"You helped too," Karina adds.

"There's no way I could have done all this without y'all," I say, looking at my best friends.

Karina nods. Daria blushes. Fire grins and says, "Never underestimate the power of Firefly Girls together."

Everybody laughs and claps.

"Exactly," I say. I straighten my shoulders and touch my blue sash. "That's why I'm proposing we help Jewel and Baby. They have a place to go when Jewel gets out of the hospital but no money to get there."

"How can we help?" Desiree asks. "We sure don't have any money."

I grin. "Yes, but we do have brownies, and that's a powerful thing."

Fire pumps her fist. "Brownie power for the greater good!"

Oh, how I wish Ree could see her!

The room fills up with excited voices.

Mrs. Bailey steps up to the podium beside me. "So what you're suggesting, Piper, is we use our brownie money this year for a service project rather than, say, a movie or a pizza party?"

Or camp up in the mountains.

I swallow that particular dream down. "Yes, ma'am," I say. "I am."

Mrs. B nods. "Okay, ladies," she says. "We'll need to take a vote. All those in favor of using brownie money this year to help Jewel and Baby, raise your hands. And remember, we don't get to keep all the money, just part of it."

"Wait," Carmen says, frowning. "We don't even know what we're voting on."

"Sure we do," Fire says. "We're voting on raising money for Jewel and Baby."

Desiree rolls her eyes. "We know that, Fire. But we don't know how *much* money."

I feel kind of sick to my stomach. This is the question I've been dreading.

"Well," I say, "the one-way bus ticket is a hundred and thirty dollars."

"That's not bad," Phoenix says. "We can raise that."

I swallow. "We'd also like to get an official emotional support animal vest for Baby, and those cost about thirty dollars."

The girls are quiet for a second. Then Angel says, "Okay, so one hundred and sixty dollars. We've done that before. I think."

I look at Mama. I do not want to say the next thing.

"Jewel also needs to put down a three-hundred-dollar deposit on the room she'll be living in at Heartwell Manor," I explain.

The whole room gasps.

"Four hundred and sixty dollars?" Alexa's eyes are as big as hubcaps. "Are you serious?"

"We'll never sell that much." Angel sighs. Heads nod in agreement.

Carmen crosses her arms over her chest. "I'd rather have a pizza party anyway."

This is not going well. I see everything I thought we'd done for Jewel and Baby slipping away. But I have to try.

"Look," I say, "I know it sounds like a lot of money—"

"It *is* a lot of money," Desiree interrupts. "And we don't even know this person. Why should we use our brownie money to help her?"

I feel my nostrils flare like Mama's. "All of us have

needed help," I say, glaring at Desiree. "All of us know what it's like to be hungry and scared, but at least we have a roof over our heads, a bed to sleep in, and *family*."

Karina stands. "Do I need to remind everyone of the Firefly Pledge? Especially," she says, looking hard at Carmen, Desiree, and Alexa, "the part where it says, 'to demonstrate kindness, compassion, fairness, and strength.'"

The room goes silent. No one will look at me or Karina.

Mrs. B steps up next to Karina. "Okay, time to vote. Remember, the vote has to be unanimous to pass. Raise your hand if you are in favor of donating our portion of brownie sales money to Jewel and Baby."

I hold my breath as one, two, then three, four, five hands go up. I feel a knot growing in my throat. I need more votes than that.

"Oh, come *on*," Fire moans. "It's an old lady and a little dog!"

Desiree crosses her arms across her chest and looks away.

Dylan, who's actually been playing quietly in the corner, pipes up, "It's Toto!"

"Oh, whatever." Desiree laughs. She raises her

hand, and so does Alexa.

I watch as another hand and another and another hand goes up.

The only holdout is Carmen.

I look right at her. "Please, Carmen?"

She looks back at me for a long time. I use all my brainpower to make her raise her hand.

Carmen looks away. Slowly she raises her hand.

Mama beams. Mrs. B grins.

Karina nods. "The motion is passed."

Fire whoops. "Yay for girl power! We're going to raise them a million bucks!"

Behind the podium where no one can see, Karina takes my hand and squeezes it.

We spend the rest of the evening dividing up the boxes of Raspberry Swirls, Mocha Mints, Buttercrunch Blondies, Choco-Lots, Caramel Dreams, and Pistachio Surprise. Mrs. B gives everybody order forms too.

"We're not going to have the luxury of time that we usually do with these order forms, ladies," Mrs. B says. "We need to get them out and the orders back by the end of next week."

Karina must see the look of panic on my face because she says, "In the meantime, we'll sell outside of the usual places. That'll be cash in hand."

"Yeah, but we won't sell enough at those places to

raise that much money," Carmen says.

Daria holds up her hand. "We won't if we just sell brownies," she says, speaking for the first time.

Phoenix snorts. "Well, what else are we going to sell?"

Daria looks at me and nods. "We'll sell Baby and Jewel's story."

Karina's eyes light up. "You hit the nail on the head. It's the story of Baby and Jewel that will sell the brownies," Karina finishes. "Not us."

"And we need to tell their story to a whole bunch of people," Fire says. "People who *love* brownies."

But how?

Mr. Yee says from the back of the room, "Isn't the monthly student assembly this Friday at Olympia Elementary?"

Karina nods. "That would be a great place to tell Jewel and Baby's story," she says. "I'll get us on the agenda."

"Who will do the telling?" Desiree asks.

All eyes turn to me. "Piper?" Karina says.

I shake my head. "No way I'm going up on that stage by myself in front of the whole school."

"You won't have to," Fire says. "We'll *all* go up on that stage with you. Right?" It's not really a question, it's a challenge.

241

Still, most of the girls look anywhere but at me.

Fire snorts. "What? Y'all afraid everyone's going to figure out you live in a shelter?"

"It's bad enough as it is," Desiree says. "Getting called all kind of names."

"It's the one place I feel like a regular kid," Phoenix explains.

It makes me mad, but on the other hand, I know how they feel. Being branded as homeless, like Ree says, makes people judge me and my family.

I see Mama and Mrs. B exchange a look.

Daria raises her chin. "So what? We may not have a house, but that doesn't mean we don't have family."

"All that matters is what *we* believe about ourselves," Karina says, looking each girl straight in the eyes.

She raises her voice, strong and sure. "We are Firefly Girls."

Carmen grins. "We *are somebody*."

Chill bumps race up and down my arms.

As one voice, we say, "And we *can* make a difference, when we shine our lights together."

∽ 46 ∾

This Jewel

Ree sits beside the bed in the light-filled room listening to her friend Jewel.

This Jewel does not talk about the voices that whisper to her, nor does she talk about the visions she has in a world filled with angels and demons.

This Jewel does not look off somewhere Ree cannot see and recite poetry to the stars.

Instead, this Jewel looks deep into Ree's dark eyes and says, "How did this happen?"

Ree holds her friend's hand and listens as Jewel talks about her life before.

The music. The students. The small house with the light-filled windows, just big enough for her, Baby, and a grand piano.

She talks about doctors, confusion, hospitals, bills that couldn't be paid. Darkness, hopelessness, suffocating sadness.

And then the letter from her sister, a ray of hope, "Come stay with me."

"And Baby too," Jewel says.

Jewel worries the edge of her blanket. "How did I lose my way? How did I forget this sister I loved?"

Ree takes her friend's hand and smooths the worry from her fingers.

She thinks about her little brother. The little brother with the bluest eyes, the lightest hair, who looked nothing like her.

Every day she wonders and worries about what became of him after she left that place called home that was not a home, a place that was not filled with love and safety but hate and hurt.

Where is he?

If he saw her flying a sign on a street corner, would he know her?

If he saw her hitching a ride, Ajax by her side, on some lonely road, would he stop?

This Jewel squeezes her friend's hand.

Ree looks into the faded blue eyes filled with hope, and fear.

"It's okay," Ree says. "It's going to be okay now, for you and Baby."

The two women, one old, one not so old, gaze out the window together and watch snow begin to fall.

∽ 47 ∾

The Edge of the World

I listen to the wind outside the window. Dylan lies curled into my side, warm as a puppy. In a few minutes, Daddy will get up and start heating water in the microwave for coffee. He'll take a shower while Mama gets us up for school.

I slip out of bed and check my backpack for brownie order forms. I want to make sure I have plenty just in case I don't have a heart attack up on the stage and die right then and there. If I do drop dead onstage, well, I don't know how Jewel and Baby will get back together.

But I'm trying, like Mama says, to look at the doughnut rather than the hole. All the good things, the possible things, the things to be grateful for.

First, after our troop meeting on Wednesday,

Daddy came home practically walking on air. "I got a car!" he announced. He picked Mama up and twirled her around. "What do you think about that, Button? A car!"

Mama's face lit up like Christmas day at the sound of her old nickname.

Dylan jumped up and down, clapping. "What kind of car, Daddy? A race car? A monster truck?"

Daddy picked up Dylan and hugged him. "Better than a race car and better than a monster truck," Daddy said, grinning. "A *free* car."

"Does it run?" I asked. How could a car that runs be free?

Daddy laughed. "Course it runs, Peeper. It runs great because *I* built the engine."

Daddy told us his boss at work had this old car that wouldn't run for nothing, but he told Daddy if he could fix it, he could have it. For free!

"So that's why you've been working so many extra hours," Mama said.

Daddy nodded. "I know it's been hard, but it'll be worth it. No more riding the bus everywhere, and," he said, "we can even leave this city if we want. Look for better opportunities somewhere else or go back to Cyprus Point."

Daddy stopped at the look on our faces.

"Or," he said, clearing his throat, "we could stay, at least for a while."

Now that Daddy has a car, he's promised to take lots of boxes of brownies to sell at work.

Second, everyone in our troop who goes to church this Sunday will tell about what we're trying to do to help Jewel and Baby. "Doesn't matter if it's a church or synagogue or a mosque," Carmen said, "on worship days, people are always more willing to part with money." Then she looked at me. "You have to be sure we all know the story to tell, though."

I did. With Daria's help on the computer, I wrote out Jewel and Baby's story and made sure each of them got a copy.

Third, when we found Ree in the park yesterday, we told her about what all we're doing to help Jewel and Baby.

"Tomorrow is a big assembly at school," Fire told her. "There'll be, like, close to a million people there."

Ree's eyes got big. "A million?"

Karina smiled. "Well, maybe not a million, but a lot. And Piper's going to tell them Jewel and Baby's story."

"And then they'll buy millions of boxes of brownies!" Fire crowed.

Ree looked at me. "You realize, don't you, that if

you tell them the whole story of Jewel and Baby, they'll probably figure out you live in a shelter?"

I nodded. "We know. But we've got to raise that money for Jewel and Baby soon. If Jewel can't go live at Heartwell Manor, nobody's sure what will happen to her, but her case worker says it probably won't include Baby."

Ree shook her head. Then she said, "If you ladies are willing to give up your brownie money to help an old woman living on the streets, then by God, we can help too."

"We?" Karina asked.

"That's right," Ree said. "I'm going to get the word out on the street. We're all going to fly our signs for Jewel."

"Do your *what*?" Fire asked.

Ree laughed. "Signs, little sister. The signs we hold up asking for help, for work, for money. We call that flying our sign."

"I will personally make sure that every person out there gives some of their money for Jewel."

"Don't they need the money for food and stuff?" I ask.

"We're all on the edge of the world," Ree said. "Lots of us have fallen off that edge with no way to get back up. If we can help one of our own get back on solid ground, into a safe place, we'll do it."

Ree walked across the park with me, Ajax by her side like always. We didn't talk but that was okay. It was a comfortable not-talking. I like that about Ree.

Then out of the blue, she said, "I saw Jewel yesterday."

I stopped and looked up at her. "You did? How is she?" I wanted to grab her hand but knew better.

Ree smiled down at me. "Better," she said. "Much better." And then, very quickly, like it was a mistake, she brushed her hand against mine.

Ree touching me, something I never thought would happen.

Daddy singing—singing!—in the shower. Something else I never, ever thought would happen here.

The doughnut. The possible. Things to be grateful for. Maybe, just maybe, we really can get Jewel and Baby home together.

❦ 48 ❦

These Girls

Ree has always been of the opinion that dogs and animals in general were the best people she knew. Ree has always thought of humans as hard-hearted animals capable of causing more pain than joy. She has never, ever trusted humans the way she trusts dogs.

But now Ree listens to these girls—fierce little Fire; tall, serious Karina; and big-hearted Piper—tell her about what they've done and all they're going to do to help an old woman they don't really know and a little dog of uncertain pedigree.

These girls who don't have homes themselves, these girls who have rarely been given a break in life, are determined to help Jewel and Baby find a home together.

These girls have hope. These girls believe they have

the power to make a difference, even if it's just for a woman and her dog.

Who is she, Ree thinks, to tell them otherwise?

Ree looks up at the sky and feels a V-shaped crack open in her heart, just like the V formed by the wild geese flying south overhead.

Who is she, she thinks, to say they can't?

~ 49 ~

A Story to Tell

It seems like about a billion sets of eyes are looking at me sitting up here on the stage at school. I was so nervous about this that I couldn't eat a bite of breakfast. Now my belly growls so loud, I'm sure they can all hear it.

Fire did. She pokes me in the side with her bony little elbow and grins. Karina, sitting on the other side of me, cuts Fire a look. I glance over at the other girls from Troop 423. None look exactly thrilled to be on stage.

"Next, Piper Trudeau and Firefly Girls Troop 423 are here to tell everybody about a special project they are working on," Randall Christiansen, our student president, says. "Let's give them our attention."

He turns and motions for me to stand up.

I think my butt is superglued to the chair.

Someone in the audience giggles.

Karina and Fire put their hands on my back and push me up.

Randall smiles. "Knock 'em dead," he says, handing me the microphone.

The rest of the girls stand and, like a swelling wave, we move into the spotlight. I look out at the faces looking up at me. Some look curious. Some look bored. Some look like they're trying to figure out why in the world they should listen to what I have to say. I hear Mama's voice from this morning say, "Everyone loves a good story, Piper. Especially one with a dog in it."

I feel my friends behind me. I relax a little. I take a deep breath. "Hi, I'm Piper Trudeau and I have a story to tell you."

"What kind of story?" some kid in the front says.

"A story about a dog and an old woman and brownies and making a difference," I say.

"Can you believe we ran out of order forms?" Fire says for the millionth time as we walk home in the snow.

"I purely can't," I say.

Karina grins. "You're a born storyteller, Piper."

A smile lights up all my insides. I've always said my superpower was selling Firefly Gourmet Brownies, but now I'm thinking it might really be in telling a story.

Daria does a happy little skip. "Your mom's going to have to get more forms *and* more boxes of brownies."

Karina nods. "I'll let her know as soon as we get home."

My heart is not quite light enough to skip, though.

"I just hope everybody gets their order forms and money back by the end of the week," I say. "We're starting to run short on time."

"Aw, don't be such a wet blanket," Fire says. "Everything's going great. Jewel's going to move to Heartwell Manor, Baby's going to be her special emotion dog, and they'll live happily ever after."

I kick at a plastic bottle. "Mama talked with Jewel's caseworker yesterday morning."

"And?" Karina asks, eyeing me.

"And," I say, not looking at them. "The hospital has agreed to keep Jewel for one week while her medication starts working again."

"But?" Karina asks, stopping.

I sigh. "*But*, that's the longest they can keep her there. If she doesn't have a place to go by Thanksgiving, she has to leave anyway."

"Where to?" Fire asks.

"Most likely to the emergency shelter," I say.

"But if Baby is her emotional support animal, he can go there too, right?" Daria asks.

"No," I say. "The emergency shelter has different rules for emotional support animals than service dogs." I sigh. "It's complicated."

"All the more reason to tell their story the best we can, then," Karina says.

When Daddy gets home from work, he grins and hands me a big wad of money. There must be a million ones and fives and tens, even a few twenties!

He laughs at my eyes, big as dinner plates. "Sold every one of those boxes of brownies, Peeper. I bet I can sell the same amount on Monday too if you can get more boxes."

"How much is it?" I ask.

Daddy shrugs. "Don't know. More than a little, I suspect."

I sit down at the table, carefully separate the bills into stacks, and start counting. I gasp. I count a second time to make sure I'm right.

"Daddy!" I say. "There's one hundred and thirty-eight dollars here!" I can hardly believe it. I quickly do the math in my head. "That only leaves us a little over three hundred dollars to raise."

Mama comes out of the bathroom, braiding her wet hair. "That's wonderful, honey. Let's put it in an envelope and take it down to Mrs. Bailey. She's the one handling the business end of this."

Riding the elevator down with Mama, I sing over and over in my head, *only three hundred more, only three hundred more.* I curl my toes inside my shoes. Our plan might actually work!

"Guess how much money Daddy gave me from brownie sales at work today?" I ask Karina, snapping my fingers with excitement when we get to their room.

Karina shrugs. She's doing her homework on her bed like I do. "Sixty dollars?"

Her little sister, Chloe, bounces on the other bed. "A million dollars!" she shouts.

I laugh. "More than sixty and less than a million."

I hand the envelope to Mrs. B. She looks at the amount Mama wrote on the outside of the envelope and whistles. "That's fantastic!"

"Yeah," I say, "and Daddy says he thinks he can sell that much again on Monday if you can get more brownies."

Mrs. B smiles. "I just got off the phone with the district troop leader. She'll be bringing over a bunch more boxes and order forms first thing tomorrow."

She takes the envelope and puts it in a metal lockbox. "This is a great start, Piper, but don't forget, we only get to keep a portion of our brownie sales money."

My heart drops down ten floors on the Elevator of

Disappointment. I'd conveniently forgotten that little fact.

I look from Mrs. Bailey to Karina. Karina shakes her head. "The National Firefly Girls Council keeps sixty percent of what we raise to cover things like the cost of the brownies, vests, badges, craft supplies, that sort of thing."

How could I have forgotten that? "Forty percent of one hundred thirty-eight dollars isn't much."

"All the more reason to keep selling brownies," Mama says.

Mrs. B touches my cheek. "Don't you worry, Piper. I'll let you know as soon as those boxes come in. We've just started."

We don't have time, though, to "just start." We've got to be over halfway done.

∽ 50 ∽

Just in Case

"You're one special boy,"
the woman at the front desk says
into Baby's ear
as he sits on her lap,
head peeking over the top of the desk,
watching people
and dogs
and cats
come and go.
There is a very big cat who is also special enough
to not be in a cage.
He sleeps in a sunny window,
and lets people pet him
even though Baby can tell
he doesn't like it.

This cat comes and goes as he pleases.
This cat does not think,
however,
that Baby is special
at all.
Baby remembers the cat named Lucky
who lived with his person
in the park.
Now that was one special cat.
The man named Brandon,
the man who has taught Baby
Sit
Stay
Down
Heel
Come
Off
says being special enough
to be in the front office
around all kinds of people
is part of his training as
Jewel's helper.
Baby has been around many different people,
sounds, smells,
while he and Jewel lived in the park
and on the streets

and once,
under a bridge.
All dogs who live outside with their people
know they must be good dogs, special dogs
to stay together.
The door opens.
The smell of winter rushes in.
A man and a small boy smile
when they see Baby at the front desk.
"Who's this special boy?"
the man asks, holding out his hand
for Baby to sniff.
"This is Baby," the woman holding him says.
"I want him!" The little boy bounces up
and down
up
and down
on his toes.
Baby sees how hungry the man's
and the boy's eyes are.
How their hands reach for him.
Baby shrinks back against the chest of the woman
holding him.
"He's not up for adoption yet," she says.
"We hope we can reunite him with his owner
soon."

Soon.
The woman takes Baby off her lap,
sits him on another chair,
slides open a drawer and
pulls out a piece of paper.
Baby watches
full of worry as
she hands it to the man and the boy
reaching for Baby.
"But just in case," she says. "Fill this out."

51

The Power of Story

It's chicken soup and grilled cheese sandwich night at the Sixth Street Community Kitchen. It's funny how normal it feels to eat here now. Everybody says hello, the volunteer servers know us by name. Even Daddy doesn't seem to mind as much as he used to.

Just then, Rick, the guy who works at the front door, comes over to our table. "I heard what you're doing for Jewel."

"You did? How?" I ask.

"Everybody on the street's talking about it. Never had something like this happen before."

He reaches into his pocket and presses a twenty-dollar bill into my hand. "This is from me for Jewel."

I feel a prickle of guilt. I always thought Rick was mean, not to let Baby and Jewel come in to eat. "That's really nice," I say.

He shrugs. "I wish I had more." Then he smiles and says, "but the volunteers are going to take up a collection. I should have more for you soon."

"Soon like tomorrow soon?" I ask.

Mama gives me a look and a little shake of her head. Rick nods, though. "Hopefully."

I cross my fingers under the table and knock on one of the wooden legs.

It's snowing that light, drifty kind of snowfall when we walk home. I like this kind of snow.

"Should have brought the car," Daddy grumbles.

Mama looks up at the sky and smiles. She loops her arm through his, "I don't mind," she says. "This is much more romantic."

Daddy snorts but he smiles too.

Dylan skips ahead, weaving in and around the snowflakes.

We come around the corner and there, standing under the streetlight in front of Hope House, are Ree and Ajax.

My heart stops with my feet. Ree's never come here at night. Ever. Has something bad happened to Jewel or Baby?

"What's wrong?" I ask.

Ree glances at Daddy and shakes back her dreadlocks.

Dylan wraps his arms around Ajax and rests his cheek on top of the big dog's silver head.

"Hi, Ree," Mama says with a smile—a real smile. Daddy nods.

Ree digs deep into her coat pocket. She stretches out her hand to me. "I brought you this."

Into my palm she drops a wad of crumpled up bills.

Daddy frowns. "Where'd that come from?"

Ree narrows her eyes. A mantle of snow rests on her shoulders and covers her long, black dreadlocks. She looks like an ice queen.

"It's not stolen, if that's what you're worried about."

Mama gives Daddy her hardest glare. "Of course that's not what we think."

Ree rolls her eyes. "I told Piper all of us who fly signs are going to give some of what we make every day for Jewel and Baby until they leave for Idaho."

Mama presses her hand to her heart. She takes the money from me and hands it back to Ree. "We can't take this, honey. Y'all need it too."

I think Ree is going to roll her eyes again, what with Mama calling her honey. But instead, she smiles with that one corner of her mouth. "We're survivors, Mrs. Trudeau."

She stuffs the money into my coat pocket and, before any of us can say anything about it, she turns and walks away into the snowy night, Ajax trotting along beside her.

Dylan pulls on my hand. "Come on, Peeper, it's movie night! Free popcorn!" We hurry inside Hope House. The whole place smells like salt and butter. Have I mentioned that popcorn is just about my favorite thing on earth?

We grab bags of popcorn and bottles of water and find four seats together. I wave to Karina and her family sitting on the other side of the room with Daria and her little brother.

"You can go sit with them, if you want," Mama says in my ear.

I shrug. "No, that's okay. I think I'll just hang out with y'all."

Sitting in the dark room, Dylan staring wide-eyed up at the screen, Mama and Daddy smiling and holding hands, I think about how different things are from a few months ago. When we lived in Cyprus Point, it was no big deal to go to a movie. I just used allowance money and went with one of my friends. Mama usually took Dylan and one of his friends to see something that was more for little kids. Daddy didn't care much for movies. He'd rather watch football or baseball on the TV.

Now that I think about it, except for eating dinner

together, we didn't do a whole lot as a family. I had my friends and my Firefly troop. Mama was either working or busy with Dylan, and Daddy worked or watched sports.

These last few months since we lost our house and had to move have been hard. Really hard. So hard, Mama sometimes cried and she and Daddy got into fights. So hard, Dylan wet the bed and took to sucking his thumb again. So hard, sometimes I've hated my life and was ashamed of what people thought of me and my family.

But sitting here in the dark like this, laughing together, sharing popcorn in our hand-me-down clothes, it's nice. It's good. I'm not ashamed of who we are and where we live.

We feel like home.

~ 52 ~

The Dog Next Door

The dog in the kennel next door to Baby
is new.
She walks slowly in on a leash.
She is too big to carry.
She has long ears,
one blue eye and one brown eye.
Baby can't help but notice that she has
a long tail with lots of long hair
that curls up at the end.
Black and brown with spots and
white paws just like Baby.
Baby pokes his nose through the wire
that separates them
and reads her story with his nose.
She is old.

She is sad.
She is confused.
Like his friend Ajax,
her joints hurt but
unlike Ajax
her heart hurts too.
The dog next door
circles once, twice,
three times and
curls up with a groan on the floor,
her side pressed against the wire.
Listen, Baby says, curling up as close as he can
to the dog next door.
Hands are kind here.
The food is good and
the water clean.
They will bring you a blanket.
And even though it smells too sweet
it is warm and
they mean well.
The dog next door
sighs a long, trembling sigh
and closes her eyes.
Listen, Baby says,
putting his nose close to hers.
They will take you out into the sun
and the wind,

not far but still
you will hear the geese fly overhead and
feel the warm sun on your fur and
smell all the delicious scents
the wind brings
and the earth holds.
And you will know there is more than
this hard floor and
wire walls.
The dog next door opens her eyes,
wags just the tip of her tail and asks,
will they come back for me?
Baby studies the dog.
Dogs can hope
but they cannot lie.
He picks up his little bunny,
the one whose fur is worn away
from love and worry,
the one who is still beloved
even though it is old and missing an eye.
He pushes it under the wire wall.
The dog next door sniffs it,
smells the comfort it holds.
She rests her silvered chin on the small bunny,
sighs
and closes her eyes.

～ 53 ～

Best Medicine

Only four days left until they make Jewel leave the hospital and go into the emergency shelter.

Angel, Alexa, Carmen, Luz, and Desiree bring the brownie money they collected on Sunday. "That story you wrote out for us made all the difference," Alexa says. "I couldn't have ever told it the way you did."

I hold my breath while Mrs. B counts the money we've brought in so far. She scribbles on a piece of paper, takes out way too much money, and then recounts what's left.

"Well, Piper," she says, "looks like you've cleared a little over two hundred dollars."

I quickly add in my head the money Mama's keeping that's come in separate from the brownie sales—Rick's donation and the money Ree brings at night from the others. That's another eighty-six dollars.

Two hundred and eighty-six dollars. That means we still need to raise at least one hundred and seventy-four more dollars by Thanksgiving.

Now we just have to hope and pray that people who ordered brownies at school bring in their forms and their money, and the people from church too. One thing I've learned over the months is what people say they'll do and what they actually *do* are often two different things. Mama says you can't let bad things make you lose your faith in humanity, though. "There are good people and bad people out there," Mama says. "Mostly good."

We'll see.

Mama comes into our room with a big smile on her face. She's been downstairs in the Resource Room filling out more job applications.

"Guess what I have, Miss Piper?" she asks, pulling my finger out of my mouth. I hadn't even realized I was chewing on my nails. There's not much of them left.

"A job?" I guess.

"Not yet," she says, "but almost as good."

She digs into the pocket of her jeans and hands me two envelopes. They both hold brownie order forms and money.

"Mama," I say, carefully stacking the bills, "where did these come from?"

She sits down on the bed beside me and studies my bitten-down fingernails. "One is from Dylan's teacher, Mrs. Harris, and the other is from Byron, downstairs. He and his husband ordered brownies for both their families. They went ahead and paid up front."

My heart lifts as I lay out the stacks of fives and tens and even a twenty. I recount again and add the two piles in my head. "I think the two orders together come to seventy-eight dollars," I say. It sure looked like a lot more when the money was in piles.

Mama must have heard the disappointment in my voice. She tucks a piece of hair behind my ear and says, "I bet your daddy will bring home more brownie money tonight."

"I sure hope so," I sigh. "Time's running out."

Mama slips an arm around me. "And I bet you're going to get lots of money for orders from your school."

"You really think so?"

Mama nods. "I really think so, Piper."

"But what if we don't get the money in time, Mama? What then?"

Mama frowns and gives me a very serious face. She shakes her finger at me. "Now Piper, what have I said?"

I blow out a breath. "I know, I know: look at the doughnut instead of the hole."

"Right," Mama says.

Mama takes my hand. "I tell you what, let's take

that money and the order forms up to Mrs. Bailey and check on Dylan. He's playing with Chloe. Then," she says, "we'll go over to the Humane Society. I think you need some Baby time."

I jump off the bed and grab Mama around the waist. "Really and truly? We're going to see Baby?"

Mama laughs. "Really and truly, baby girl. I've got the car today. We'll go see Baby and then pick up your father." She touches the tip of my nose with her finger. "How does that sound?"

"It sounds like the *best* medicine!"

~ 54 ~

Baby and Piper

Baby's heart leaps with joy
when he smells the girl
coming toward his cage.
His white paws dance
Tap tap tap
on the cold concrete floor.
A tremble of excitement starts
at the tip of his tail and,
by the time it reaches the tip of his nose,
his body wiggles and waggles all over.
The girl! He yips with happiness.
My girl! He barks for all to hear.
The girl smiling, reaching out to touch his nose.
"Hi, you," she says. "Hi, Baby boy."
He remembers when she came here
when he was scared and lost.

She said his name,
then too,
reminding him who he is and
who has his heart.
Now she comes inside his cage.
He crawls into her lap
and covers her face with kisses because
he is so, so happy to smell her and
because he can feel
the worry in her heart.
His Jewel had that worry in her heart too
and it was Baby's most important job
to take that worry away.
Baby leaps from the girl's lap and
twirls on his back legs.
Just like Jewel, the girl laughs
and claps her hands and
just like that
the dark smell of worry
is gone.
A woman
not much taller than the girl
with a similar scent
says, shall we go out into the sun?
Baby sees she holds two leashes in her hand.
The woman hands one leash to the girl.
The woman's hand smells like love and

peanut butter.
Baby watches with boundless curiosity
and hope
as the woman opens the door to
the kennel next door and clips a leash on the old dog
whose eyes are filled with small bits of hope.
Together
they leave the inside
for the outside
Girl
Baby
Woman
Dog Next Door
and turn their faces up
to the bright sun.

༺ 55 ༻

Apprehension

Every day, money is trickling in. Daddy's brought home money from work the last two days, and every night Rick gives me money collected at the Sixth Street Community Kitchen.

And when we come back from supper, Ree and Ajax are always waiting on the corner with more she's collected from her family of sign flyers—that's what Daddy calls them. "I don't think I'll ever look at them the same," he says. I won't either.

But there's no two ways around it: time's getting short. Very short.

When I got home from school yesterday, Byron had a package for me: Baby's emotional support vest. Byron ordered it on his credit card since we don't have one.

I opened up the box and held the vest up for Byron to see.

"It looks very official," Byron said, admiring the red and black colors, and fingering the buckles. "Well made too. He'll be able to wear this for a long time."

"I hope so," I said. Time's not just running out for Jewel, it's running out for Baby too. Tamara at the Humane Society said more and more people have filled out applications to adopt Baby. "He won't have any trouble finding a great home if things don't work out," she said.

"But you said you'd keep him until Jewel gets out of the hospital."

"We can keep him a few days longer," Tamara had said, "but that's it. There are other dogs needing his kennel space, Piper."

I feel sick remembering all this as I climb onto the school bus.

"Hey, Piper!" Jerome waves from the back, where he sits with Noah. They're both grinning.

"What's up?" I ask, plopping down on the seat in front of them.

"This!" Jerome hands me an envelope filled with money and two brownie order forms.

My jaw drops. "That looks like a lot of money." I gasp.

"My track team *loves* Firefly Gourmet Brownies,

especially Coach Sloan," he explains. "Can't get enough of those Mocha Mint and Choco-Lots."

Noah hands me another envelope. "It's not as much," he says shyly, "but every little bit counts."

"It surely does," I say. I hold both envelopes to my heart. "Y'all are the *best*."

Walking down the hall to my class, I notice more kids are smiling at me. One boy even calls me Brownie Girl. Is it the magic power of brownies and story, or am I finally seeing the whole doughnut?

All day at school, kids and teachers turned in money and order forms to Vice Principal Meeks. As soon as the end-of-school bell buzzed, Karina and I raced down to the office to pick them up.

"Hope you brought a wheelbarrow," Mr. Meeks says with a grin.

"No kidding," Karina says, staring at the box full of cash and forms.

Me, I can't say a word. It seems too good to be true.

Usually, me, Daria, Karina, and Fire walk home from school, but today, we ride the bus. No dawdling today: we've got money to count.

I'm still tongue-tied with excitement and worry when we get to Karina's family's room.

We hold our breath as Mrs. Bailey opens the box.

"My goodness," she says. She pushes the box toward us. "Well, girls, get counting."

"It's got to be a million dollars at least," Fire says.

"Actually, it's got to be at least one hundred and seventy-four dollars," Karina reminds us.

Fire and I separate the bills into stacks of ones, fives, tens, and twenties. I can't believe how many twenties there are.

Then Fire and I count it out.

"Holy cow," Fire says.

Daria counts it again, then writes the total on a piece of paper: $246.

I nearly jump all the way up to the ceiling. "We did it! We did it and then some!"

"Piper, honey, don't forget we only get to keep forty percent of that," Mrs. B says.

Daria groans.

Karina does the math. "We get to keep ninety-eight dollars."

My heart crashes to the floor.

But then I remember: there's the money Mama's collected from Ree and Rick at the Sixth Street Community Kitchen and the rest of the brownie money.

I call Mama. It only takes two blinks of an eye for

her and Dylan to come down with the other money.

Before Mrs. B starts counting again, I say, "Wait." I take my Band-Aid box out of my pack and pull out my allowance. "Add this in too."

It seems like it takes Mrs. B forever and ever to do a final count. I feel apprehension—a new word we learned today—growing inside me. Will it be enough? And if it's not, what do we do?

I almost bust with that apprehension when she recounts the money *two more times*!

"Oh, come *on*," Fire moans.

Finally, Mrs. Bailey writes something on a piece of paper. She shows it to Mama and sighs.

"Well, girls," Mrs. B says, shaking her head. "You sure did give it your best, especially you, Piper."

My heart drops to the absolute, most putrid basement of disappointment. Tears prick my eyes.

And then a huge grin splits her face. "And it sure did pay off: you ladies raised five hundred eighty-six dollars and seventy-nine cents!"

We all look at each other, not believing what we just heard.

"Wait," I say, "how much of that do we get to keep for Jewel and Baby?"

Mrs. B gives my shoulder a squeeze. "You get to keep *all* of it, Piper."

Quick, I do the math in my head.

"*And,*" I whisper in case it isn't true, "we have one hundred and twenty-six dollars *over* what we need?"

Mama grins. "And seventy-nine cents."

Fire digs into the pocket of her jeans. She drops a penny into the pile of change. "Make that eighty cents."

"We did it, Piper!" Daria says, hugging me.

And then we hug, all of us together—me, Mama, Karina, Fire, Daria, and Mrs. B—laughing and crying good tears.

Finally, we untangle. Karina glances at the clock.

Her mother nods. "We've got phone calls to make, and quick."

✎ 56 ✎

His Jewel

Baby hears the door open.
He sits up.
It is not the usual time to eat.
It is not the usual time to go outside.
Dogs bark and bellow their greetings
of hope.
Footsteps hurry toward him.
He looks to the empty space next door.
But she is no longer there.
She and the little brown bunny
went to a new home,
a forever home,
where they will love her
silver face and soothe
her aching bones.

Then Baby smells an almost
most wonderful smell:
the girl!
She has come back!
Baby jumps against her legs
and yips his happiness.
She scoops him up,
kisses the top of his head,
and carries him out
into the sunlit lobby.
The room is filled with faces
all smiling
(except that cat)
at him.
The man named Brandon.
The woman named Tamara.
The man whose gentle hands
feed him, take him out
into the sunlight.
The woman who smells like the girl
he has come to love.
Still,
Baby searches for the face,
the particular smell of the one
who holds his heart with hers
but he does not find her there.

His ears droop.
His bit of a tail sags
with disappointment.
The girl sets him down on the floor.
"Look, Baby," she says.
"Look what I have for you."
Gently she wraps a red and black vest
across Baby's back and chest
and under his belly.
He hears the click click of buckles.
It smells different from the fleece coat
Jewel wraps him in when he's cold.
This coat sits on Baby's shoulders
in a way Baby has never felt before.
Important.
Everyone in the sunlit room claps and smiles.
Baby can feel how happy they are and
he thinks he should be happy too.
But none of these faces is the one
his soul needs.
None are his Jewel.
The girl clips a leash onto his vest
and says his two favorite words.
"Let's go!"
But for the first time ever, Baby hesitates.
For the first time he asks, "Where?"

✺ 57 ✺

Serendipity

I'm sitting in the back seat of our car on the way to Mercy Memorial Hospital with Baby on my lap.

Even through the official emotional support animal vest he's wearing, I can feel his big, little heart beating against my palm. I love the weight of him on my legs, and his salty smell, the feel of his breath on my hand as he looks, panting, out the window.

I run a hand along his back. His little tail wags. How can my heart be so happy and so sad all at the same time?

"What do you think is in here?" Dylan asks.

He's been itching to unzip the duffel bag the folks at the Humane Society gave Baby as a going-away present.

I shrug. "I don't know. Let's take a look."

I unzip the bag—a lot smaller than the one of

Jewel's that Baby stayed with in the park all that time—and look inside. A water bowl, bottled water, treats, a blanket, a brush, his medical records, and papers showing he's an official emotional support animal.

"Boring," Dylan decides.

"Yes, but things he'll need for the trip to Idaho," Mama says from the front seat.

His little bunny toy isn't in here though. I look all through the bag but can't find it. "Dang," I say.

"What's wrong?" Dylan asks.

"Baby's stuffed bunny isn't in here."

Dylan frowns. "Does he love his bunny the way I love Ted the Shark?"

"Yeah," I say. "He kind of does."

Daddy smiles, looking at us in the rearview mirror. "I doubt he'll even remember, once he sees Jewel."

Daddy swings the car into the parking lot at Mercy Memorial and parks the car.

"Maybe you should wait here with Baby," he says to me.

"He's probably allowed in, though," I say, "now that he's her emotional support dog." At least I hope so.

We walk into the lobby, Baby leading the way.

Mama says to the lady at the front desk, "We're here to pick up Jewel Knight. She's being discharged today."

The lady frowns over her glasses at Baby. "It," she says through her nose, "is *not* allowed."

Before I can say anything, Daddy says in his low, soft voice, "Beg your pardon, ma'am, but he is." He picks Baby up. "He's an official support animal, like the vest says." When Daddy uses that voice, you don't argue.

The nurse looks from Baby to Daddy. "The patient is being discharged today?"

Daddy nods. "Yes, ma'am."

She waves her hand, shooing us away. "Go on up," she says, "but don't linger."

When we get up to the floor where Jewel is, Baby knows exactly where he is. He pulls on the leash and whimpers. His little tail wiggles like crazy. I can't believe it, but he heads straight for Jewel's room!

Daddy pushes open the door. Jewel is sitting on the hospital bed, her back to us, talking with her case worker.

Ms. Madison's face lights up. "Well, look who's here!"

Baby throws back his little head and lets out the biggest bark.

Jewel turns around and gasps. Her face lights up like Christmas, Fourth of July, and a birthday cake with a thousand candles, all rolled together. "Baby!" she cries.

Baby pulls the leash from my hand and, in two giant leaps I would never have thought that little dog could manage, he's on the bed and in Jewel's arms. His furry front paws wrap around Jewel's neck; his tongue licks and licks the tears streaming down Jewel's cheeks.

"He's just like a little person," Mama says with wonder.

I look over at Daddy, who's busying himself with the wheelchair. I don't know that anybody else sees it, but I do. I see a tear slide down his cheek.

The Country-Wide bus station is surprisingly busy for it being the middle of the day. All kinds of people are coming and going. I was so scared and angry and confused when my family came through here, but this time I'm happy to be back.

Jewel stands in between Mama and Ree, clutching her bus ticket in one hand and Baby in the other. Ree promised that no matter what, she'd be here. One thing I've learned about Ree through all this is she's someone you can count on. Even if she does have tattoos, dreadlocks, and a ring in her eyebrow.

A voice announces over the loudspeaker the bus to Boise is leaving in two minutes.

Daddy touches Jewel's arm. "Let me take these over to the bus for you, Miss Knight." He picks up her black suitcase and duffel bag.

Jewel turns to Ree and hugs her long and hard. They look into each other's eyes—sparkling blue into coal black. They don't say anything, but you can tell they're saying all they need to about what they've seen and what they know.

Jewel takes Mama's hand and squeezes it. "I don't know how I can ever thank you for all your many kindnesses."

Before Mama can answer, Jewel turns to me and touches my face. "And you, dear Piper," she says, "are purely a wonder."

"It wasn't just me, though," I say. "I couldn't have done it without my friends."

Jewel smooths her hand over my hair. "Yes, but you, you *saw*. Not just with your eyes, but with your heart."

I reach into my coat pocket and hand Jewel a small white photograph.

"I forgot I had this," I say. It's the one of her and Sis, arms slung around each other, kicking up their heels.

She looks at it and smiles. Then she lets out a big laugh. "Oh, I remember this! Sis and I could be so silly!"

"All aboard!" The bus driver calls.

Jewel turns to me and smiles. "Would you carry Baby for me, Piper?"

I take Baby into my arms and hold him close. He licks my chin and wags his tail about a mile a minute.

We walk out to the bus in the falling snow.

"Don't forget to call Mrs. Tooney tomorrow, Jewel. She's expecting you," Jewel's case worker says. She's already got a new social worker all lined up for Jewel in Boise.

Daddy hands Baby's duffel bag up to Jewel as she stands on the bottom step of the bus.

It about tears me up to do it, but I place Baby in Jewel's arms.

Jewel raises Baby's paw and waves it. "Say goodbye to all the good people, Baby."

Baby yips and sneezes.

I laugh, but my heart is breaking too. I love that little dog, I surely do. I am so happy Baby and Jewel can be together, but a corner of my heart still wishes like anything he was mine.

One last time, Jewel wipes a tear from her face. "This will be the best Thanksgiving I could have ever wished for," she says.

And then the bus doors close, and they're gone.

I can't hardly believe it. All these weeks of think-ing about Jewel and especially Baby day and night, and it's done. Over. I'll never see them again.

My heart feels like someone yanked it out and wrung it like a washcloth.

Then I feel a small, sticky hand slip into mine. Dylan looks up at me and says in his croaky little voice, "It's okay, Peeper."

As we start back to the car, Daddy and Ree walking side by side, Mama stops. She looks at the hand of Dylan's I'm not holding. "Where's Ted the Shark?" she asks, kind of in a panic because we all know what a fit Dylan can pitch when he's lost Ted the Shark.

Dylan grins, showing the gap left by the tooth he lost just the other day. "I put him in Baby's duffel bag. It's a surprise."

I laugh. The sadness in my heart untwists and lifts. I tweak his ear. "You're something else, Toto, you know that?"

As we walk back to our car, I remember that word: serendipity. It means when things that don't seem to have anything to do with each other come together in a good way. Kind of like puzzle pieces that don't look like anything until you put them together and all of a sudden you have a tree or the sky. It was serendipity, that day I saw Jewel and Baby on the street corner, and it was serendipity meeting Ree in the park, moving to Hope House and finding the best friends I've ever had and the best Firefly Girls troop ever. All the pieces coming together to help Jewel and Baby. And me.

If you ask me, I think there's a little bit of magic in serendipity too.

I look at the snow-covered mountains rising up so high, so sharp in the distance. Daddy says come spring, we'll go up there and see all there is to see: the forests and streams and lakes. I reckon that means we're here to stay.

Until then, me and the girls of Troop 423 will shine our little lights together to make the world a better place, even if it's just for an old woman and her little dog. Because to Jewel and Baby—and to us—it means everything in the world.

~ 58 ~

Baby and Jewel

Baby knows the smell of the bus.
The sharp, slick smell of gas,
the sweet scent of the fake leather seats,
the salty musk of people
riding the bus together.
Baby hears the engine roar to life.
"Let's go!" he yips
but it is a quiet yip because Baby knows
he is not only a good, good dog,
but an important dog too.
He feels the rhythm of the rocking bus,
and the hum of the wheels.
But this time,
this time,
Baby rides in Jewel's lap

instead of inside a dark duffel bag.
This time
Baby looks out the window at the world
passing by.
This time he does not hear fear
in Jewel's voice as she talks
to someone not there.
This time she talks to him,
whispers in his ear about
the piano she will play,
the sister who will love him
almost as much as she does.
She smiles as she describes sun
coming in windows,
a soft bed,
and warm blankets.
Jewel runs her hand over the red and black vest
Baby wears like a superhero cloak
across his shoulders and chest.
She laughs just a little as she fingers the badges
the girls from Firefly Troop 423
sewed on Baby's vest.
One for Animals.
One for Adventure.
And one for Helping.
"Sis says not to expect too much,

that Heartwell Manor is nothing fancy."
Jewel hugs Baby to her.
"We don't need much," I told her,
"as long as we're together."
Baby licks Jewel's chin and
wags his bit of a tail.
He sneezes in agreement once,
then again.
He listens as Jewel hums softly under her breath.
He watches the world slide past the window
as the road spools out ahead.
A world full of wonder
and hope. And love.
Baby and Jewel,
a pack of two,
warm and safe together
again.

AUTHOR'S NOTE

On a cold, windy day, my husband and I were running our usual errands in downtown Salt Lake City. As always, we saw many homeless folks "flying signs" on street corners and at busy intersections, asking for help. Like most people, I looked straight ahead or occasionally offered a dollar or two.

Then I saw them at an intersection: an old woman with long silver hair and a faded flowered dress, a little dog sitting by her feet. I was struck by the look of utter desperation on the woman's face as she held up her sign. But the dog (who looked very much like Toto) looked calmly at the mountains in the distance, content as could be. The light changed. We moved on. But I could not get that woman and her dog out of my mind.

Thus began several years of research and volunteer work. I wanted to understand why so many people lived on the streets. What happened to people like that woman who had a dog? Could she go into a shelter? What were their stories?

I learned through research and volunteering that

there are many reasons a person or family could be living without a home—domestic violence, job loss, medical expenses, addiction, mental illness. Like Piper said, it's often a combination of events that brings everything crashing down. At any given time, over 500,000 people in this country are homeless and over 30 percent of those are families with children. Yet every story is different.

The inspiration for Piper's Firefly troop is Girl Scout Troop 6000 in the New York borough of Queens. One evening, after I had started writing Baby and Piper's story, I saw a piece on national news about this remarkable Girl Scout troop. Just like all Girl Scout troops, Troop 6000 goes on field trips, earns merit badges, learns leadership skills, and shares its ups and downs. But unlike most girls in scouting, the girls in Troop 6000 live in a shelter for families experiencing homelessness.

At the end of the story on the news, one of the girls in Troop 6000 said, "As the Girl Scouts have taught me, no matter who you are, where you live, or what your situation is, we're all equal." I knew Piper was going to need a group like that. Girl Scouts of America also knew that more girls and their families living in shelters needed troops too. Since Girl Scout Troop 6000 was established in early 2017, fifteen more shelters now have Girl Scout troops, and more are being established throughout the country.

It is my great good hope that through Piper and Baby's story, you, the reader, will see those people on the street corners flying their signs just a little bit differently. When you see that person experiencing homelessness with a dog or cat, you'll know that animal is the most important connection in that person's life. And when you hear that new kid in your class lives in a shelter, you'll know that, just like you, they want to feel like they belong.

To find out how you can help, check out the following organizations:

- Pets of the Homeless:
  www.petsofthehomeless.org
- The Street Dog Coalition:
  www.thestreetdogcoalition.org
- National Alliance to End Homelessness:
  www.endhomelessness.org
- The Coalition for the Homeless:
  www.coalitionforthehomeless.org
- National Center on Family Homelessness:
  www.air.org/center/national-center-family-homelessness

As Linda said, everybody needs to feel like they have another heartbeat on their side.

ACKNOWLEDGMENTS

During the journey that would become this book, I have been so fortunate to have many heartbeats on my side.

To my bighearted agent, Alyssa Eisner Henkin, thanks as always for believing in the story I just had to tell.

I am once again so grateful to have had Maria Barbo and Katherine Tegen Books on my side. Maria, you always ask the right questions.

Huge thanks to the HarperCollins team—Megan Gendell, Jon Howard, Stephanie Guerdan—for making sure I look like I know what I'm doing, even when I don't. Y'all keep me honest.

Artist Erwin Madrid, thank you for creating such a beautiful image of Baby for the jacket cover! Doubtless it will grab everyone's heart.

Many thanks to Vikki Terrile and Dr. Julie Ann Winkelstein for your thoughtful reading of an early draft of *Stay*. Because of your suggestions, I know my story is a much more respectful and rich depiction of people and families experiencing homelessness. Thank you for all you do in your own lives to make the world a better place.

Two books were particularly important to me in understanding the world of families experiencing homelessness and the pets of the homeless: *Invisible Nation: Homeless Families in America*, by Richard Schweid (University of California Press, 2016) and *My Dog Always Eats First: Homeless People and Their Animals*, by Leslie Irvine (Lynn Rienner Publishers, 2015). Thank you for helping me understand.

I will always have these names on my Grateful list: Jean Reagan, Lora Koehler, Chris Graham, Becky Hall, and Charlene Brewster. True hearts all.

And to my husband, Todd, who helps me see the doughnut rather than the hole, always.

Don't miss
A Pup Called Trouble

1

Eyes Wide Open

On an early spring day, in a den tucked beneath the roots of an old oak tree, four coyote pups were born.

During the first week, they nursed and slept just like all newborn puppies do.

All except one.

Unlike the other pups, one member of the Singing Creek Pack was born with eyes wide open and ears—no bigger than thumbnails—twitching with curiosity.

He heard the *shhh, shhh, shhh* of the wind wandering in the trees. He turned toward the *caw! caw!* of a crow. His blue eyes widened. Light! Light dappled by leaves danced above and beyond.

With a tiny squeak of excitement, the coyote pup

left the warmth of his sleeping mother's side. He scrabbled and stumbled on wobbly legs across the cool dirt floor of the den and up the tunnel toward the light.

With one last scramble, the little pup pulled himself up and emerged, blinking, from the den. He sat on his fat rump and lifted his tiny nose to the air. So many scents! Not his mother's deep, comforting musk or the milky sweetness of his brother and sisters or the rich, dark smell of the earth.

Here was the scent of green leaves just unfurling, the sap rising in the trees. Here, the air was rich with the smell of feathers, fur, tiny green shoots pushing up through wet ground and the last pools of snow.

He stood and turned his ears toward a sound: a faint rustling in the grass. He wiggled his nose. Something warm and furry scratched in the dirt. The little coyote trembled with barely contained excitement. Although the pup was only days old, thousands of years of coyote instinct coursed through his veins. He was, after all, a hunter.

The pup took one step and then another out into the sunlight. He closed his eyes against the unaccustomed bright, so he did not see the great, wide form of an eagle flying low across the meadow.

But he did hear the bloodcurdling hunting cry of the bird.

The pup squealed in fear. He turned to run back to the safety of the den.

He felt the *swoosh* of the enormous bird's wings. He looked up into fierce, hungry eyes, something he would never forget. The pup pressed his belly against the ground as the eagle hurtled toward him.

"No!" came an angry bark.

The pup's father hurled himself between his son and the eagle. The eagle's outstretched talons scraped across the shoulders of the larger coyote.

The pup watched in amazement as his father wheeled and, with barely the flick of an ear, leaped up and grabbed the eagle by the tail feathers.

The eagle screamed in outrage. With one mighty beat of his wings, he pulled free of the coyote and climbed into the sky.

Father coyote sniffed his son from tip to tail. Satisfied that he was unhurt, he gently nipped the small pup. "What in the name of Mother Moon are you doing out here?"

The pup was too young, life too new, to explain what drew him from the safety of his mother's side. He looked up and up into his father's yellow eyes and simply said, "I wanted to see."

The father snorted. He picked up his son by the scruff of his neck and carried him down into the den.

Mother coyote woke at the sound of paws on the dirt. She leaped to her feet. With one bound, she grabbed the pup from her mate and carried him back to his mewling brother and sisters.

Father plopped down with a sigh.

Mother sniffed her little wanderer. "I knew when this one was born with his eyes open," she said, tucking him firmly under her paws, "he was going to be all kinds of trouble."